Aloha And Mai Tais

A Novel About Hawaii
In The 1930's and 1940's.

Rosemary I. Patterson

Copyright © 2002 by Rosemary I. Patterson.

ISBN :   Softcover   1-4010-4731-9

All rights reserved. No part of this book may be reproduced or transmitted in any form or by any means, electronic or mechanical, including photocopying, recording, or by any information storage and retrieval system, without permission in writing from the copyright owner.

This is a work of fiction. Names, characters, places and incidents either are the product of the author's imagination or are used fictitiously, and any resemblance to any actual persons, living or dead, events, or locales is entirely coincidental.

This book was printed in the United States of America.

To order additional copies of this book, contact:
Xlibris Corporation
1-888-795-4274
www.Xlibris.com
Orders@Xlibris.com

Contents

Acknowledgements. 7
Chapter 1.
    Atherton Scully. 9
Chapter 2.
    Investment Gamble. 18
Chapter 3.
    Kimi Kai'ika. 23
Chapter 4.
    Teri'i And Ito. 30
Chapter 5.
    Music Director In Paradise. 33
Chapter 6.
    Compromise. 44
Chapter 7.
    Mission International. 53
Chapter 8.
    Passing On The Old Music. 62
Chapter 9.
    The Revue. 81
Chapter 10.
    Opening Night. 89
Chapter 11.
    Repercussions. 96
Chapter 12.
    Hotel Bookings Slow. 109

Chapter 13.
: Complications. 113
Chapter 14.
: Guatemala. 124
Chapter 15.
: Disillusionment. 132
Chapter 16.
: Changes. 137
Chapter 17.
: Journey To California. 141
Chapter 18.
: On The Mainland. 146
Chapter 19.
: Return to the Tropical Palace. 151
Chapter 20.
: Martial Law. 156
Chapter 21.
: On The Mainland. 163
Chapter 22.
: Forced Changes. 169

Acknowledgements.

A big thank you to my husband, Nick Patterson, for his photo of the Aloha Tower on Oahu and his never-ending support of my writing projects. Many thanks to our daughter Catherine Patterson-Sterling, M.A., for her creative suggestions for this novel.

Chapter 1.

Atherton Scully.

I sighed deeply as I stood and surveyed the expensive, polished marble bust of my half-uncle, Damon Scully, in the prestigious, Honolulu cemetery. It was 1932 in the United States Territory of Hawaii and Damon Scully had been dead for ten years. But to me his voice had never been completely stilled. I sighed as I could swear I could hear him calling me "Boy" from below the carefully cultivated grass of his plot.

There were very few things that I had ever done in my life that had managed to please Uncle Damon when he was living. And now he was hounding me from the grave. I certainly had not been pleasing him for the last ten years. I had not only failed to regain a position of power in one of the companies that controlled ninety-nine percent of Hawaii's business but I had already lost over half of the money he had left to my wife and his daughter Jessica.

I was still one of the wealthiest persons in Honolulu thanks to my wife who had inherited her father's and my uncle's fortune. Unfortunately the money was in the grasp of Jessica's well-manicured, red nails and she wouldn't free it anymore for risky business ventures. Risky business ventures were the only kind of business ventures I could take part in thanks to my blacklisting ten years previously by Honolulu's notorious business oligarchy.

My close association with Hawaii's Delegate to Congress had ended at his death and I had no longer been useful to the oligarchy.

The oligarchy controlled Hawaii's land, business, and power. It consisted mainly of descendents of the Calvinist missionaries who convinced Hawaii's King Kamehameha III to put all the land in the Islands up for grabs in 1850. The missionaries and their descendents, of course, took full advantage of one of the greatest land sales in the history of western civilization. Native Hawaiians, who had no money and no way of earning it, lost everything. Missionary descendents and other westerners turned the Islands into a giant sugar-cane plantation. Not satisfied with owning all the land, the 'Missionary Party,' as deposed Queen Lili`uokalani liked to refer to them, grabbed what was left of Sovereignty in Hawaii. In 1893, they overthrew a legal Constitutional Monarch with treaties of independence to major world powers by arranging the placement of Marines off the U.S.S. Boston. The Marines, by order of the U.S. Minister Stevens, were placed between the Queen and the business leaders seeking her overthrow. Should she have fired it would have been tantamount to declaring war on the U.S.

My wife Jessica was a rarity. She was a highly-sexed beauty in an age where most Honolulu society matrons still recoiled in horror from the subject of men's favorite activity. I was eternally thankful for such a physical woman. But I could not believe in the change to Jessica's personality since her father's death. Before his demise and my firing by one of Honolulu's foremost entrepreneurs, and particularly before my last three failed business deals, she had left all the business details to me. Now, she questioned me about even trivial matters concerning our finances. I had been noticing recently that she was becoming more and more like her dead father all the time.

Sometimes, to my absolute horror, the old man, himself, seemed to be speaking through Jessica's facial expressions and voice.

I glanced at Damon Scully's epitaph at the base of his statue.

"Sugar Is King In Hawaii," I read aloud to Jessica. My wife looked very desirable in the tropical lushness of the cemetery that day. She was dressed in a fashionably-tight, Hawaiian print dress that accented her voluptuous figure perfectly. Her flaming, red hair had still not greyed and I knew she looked much younger than myself with my already greying sideburns. I looked for a hiding spot where I could demonstrate my amorous longings. Several risky, business ventures had failed and my failures were generalizing over to my prowess in bed. Recently I hadn't been in the mood and Jessica was asking me what the trouble was.

"Maybe behind that mausoleum," I speculated. "Damn, there's someone tending the Anthuriums." I returned my thoughts to Uncle Damon's epitaph.

> "Sugar Is King In Hawaii. No one understood this better than Damon Scully, Jan. 13, 1836 to Jan. 21, 1922. His distinguished career led to the triumph of the sugarcane industry and many of it's finest accomplishments."

"No doubt dictated by Uncle Damon himself, eh Dear?" I said sarcastically as I, at least, recognized the arrogance in her father's epitaph. However, Jessica seemed to miss my sarcasm completely. I gasped as her facial expression reminded me of the one her dead father used when he was about to set me straight.

"Of course, Atherton," she replied. My ears shrieked. "How can she sound just like him?" I thought, gasping.

"My father never doubted for one moment his mission in life. He always felt he was predestined to take the lands of Hawaii and make them more productive. How well he succeeded. If only you could be more like him, Boy."

I reeled. She had called me "Boy." The only people in the world that ever addressed me by that insulting term was old Damon and my former business partner, Michael Bridgewater. Jessica knew how much I hated it when either one of them used to call me "Boy."

"What do you mean? You want me to be more like your father?" I stood up and sucked in the slight pot around my middle. I'd been much too sedentary lately, I realized.

"Why I'm sure our prestigious mansion and our extensive land holdings on the Islands are evidence of worth in the eyes of the Divine? Aren't they evidence of worthiness in the eyes of my wife?" Jessica was an avowed Calvinist. I tried to use the Church's line that material signs of wealth were a sure sign of admission into the elite predestined for Heaven.

"Oh, for Heaven's sake. You've been so sensitive lately. I only wish you had even one-quarter of my father's self-confidence."

"Many would have said that your father was arrogant, not self-confident."

"Don't you dare critize my father. I'm beginning to think that it was only his advice that made us as wealthy as we are. How can you go on kidding yourself? Look how you've withdrawn from public view ever since the last business failure."

My heart sank as Jessica's criticism stung deeply. I hadn't realised my wife was tiring of the self-doubt I'd been experiencing since my well-connected business partner of twenty years had dumped me and everything I had touched since had collapsed.

"If only you would support me in this new business venture, Dear," I tried to stop her accusing voice. I couldn't look at her facial expressions. If Jessica turned on me too, I realised I would be finished financially. Most of our remaining wealth was in her name.

"If only it was clear what line of business to go into now?" Jessica continued her onslaught. "So much has changed since the stock market crash."

Fear shot through my spine as my wife reacted by staring hostilely at me.

"She's looking at me just like her father again. Just before he would ask: "You stupid or something,Boy?" I went into some kind of severe reaction. For the first time I was realising how much like her father Jessica was.

"You stupid or something, Boy? Get that silly look off your face." I reeled. It was like deja vu. For over twenty years I'd put up with Damon Scully and Michael Bridgewater berating me like a common cur. Now my wife seemed to be filling the void of their absences. Despite the eighty-three degree heat and the tropical humidity the blood drained from my face.

"If only you would let me make one final investment, Jessica," I whined.

"No wonder my father left everything in my name?" I couldn't bear to look directly in my wife's eyes. They looked eerily like her fathers. "Your failed business ventures have cost millions."

"Let me invest in that luxury hotel in Waikiki, the Tropical Paridise." I tried again to convince my wife to back me in another venture.

"You know that the Tropical Palace Hotel has gone into receivership, don't you, Dear? God knows that Theodore Wiltshire's been phoning me for weeks now about it. It can be had for ten cents on the dollar."

"What makes you think that's such a good investment, Boy?" I gasped as I could swear that Damon Scully's voice was coming through my wife's throat. I knew I had to get my normal control of my wife back. Before her father's death she had never questioned anything I did.

"Some say that tourism will be flat until the depression on the mainland is over. Besides, I'm beginning to think that maybe father was right all those years ago—that you really don't have much of a backbone. But maybe you do have something this time?" Jessica looked like she just remembered something she had heard lately.

"Strike while the iron is hot, Father always said. Maybe you are right this time? Michael Bridgewater himself, told me he is thinking of investing in that hotel."

"When did Bridgewater tell you that Jessica?" I couldn't believe she was still in contact with the scroundrel.

"How do you know what he's going to invest in?"

My worst fears shot to the surface. "Maybe she and Bridgewater were becoming lovers again," I thought with a growing feeling of despair. I knew my former partner had never completely lost his fondness for the woman I had stolen from him. Every so often he and Jessica developed a discreet affair.

"Surely she has more loyalty towards me than that?" My thoughts galloped off into Paranoia. "I never thought my own wife would be civil to Bridgewater again after what he did." Jessica must have sensed my thoughts. Her voice rose even more.

"Really, you can't expect me to avoid Michael and his wife. Why they're the cream of the crop of Honolulu society. Just because you lack a backbone and have gone into some kind of retreat from the world don't expect me to come along with you and lie cowering. I have our children to think of as well as my reputation."

"Our children deserve the careers and lifestyles they're entitled to even if their father was publicly humiliated and hasn't managed to keep a new business venture running for anymore than two years since."

I sighed deeply "It's the children she's thinking of," I decided, "not her old beaux." But I knew the risk of what I was proposing to Jessica was huge.

"What if I fail again?" I worried. "Why it could be years before big money would be made out of tourism."

Jessica must have sensed my hesitation.

"Atherton," she reasoned. "If I go into that hui for the new Hotel in Waikiki we'll have to sink in all our capital. We might even have to float a loan if the Hotel can't be expected to make a profit for the first while. We would have to mortgage our house and your property on the Islands. We could lose everything we own. Are you sure you want me to invest more of our money? Shouldn't we just be satisfied with the substantial rental income we get from our real-estate investments?"

"Risk is how your relatives and Bridgewaters got to be where they are today," I argued. "Your father always floated loans for his enterprises. How do you think he accumulated the fortune he did. By investing in Government bonds or something?"

I was having a hard time convincing Jessica. I realised myself I wasn't sure I wanted to go into as big a gamble as the Tropical Palace venture would demand. But my ego was spurring me on. It wouldn't let me relax. I had to prove myself in business again. I tried to think of another way to get Jessica to come up with some of her reserve capital.

"I'll try reverse Psychology," I thought. I decided to take advantage of my wife's enculturation about the inferiority of Native Hawaiians. She was one of the most condemning of the missionary descendents I had ever come into contact with.

"But maybe you are right about this investment, Dear," I tried to keep my voice casual. "Maybe tourism isn't the way to go," I switched my tactics. "Why, Iwana Keaka assures me that the growth of the tourist industry in the Islands is one more nail in the coffin of Hawaii's original people and their culture. He says that the portrayal of Hawaiian women as scantily-clad, sexually alluring sirens in the tourist literature is insulting. And that the expectation that Hawaiian men are fit to be no more than surfers, porters, and beach boys is severely limiting the upward mobility of Hawaiians."

My words seemed to incense my wife.

"Iwana Keaka, that left-over, Hawaiian coutier from King Kalakaua's time, you're listening to him!" she shouted. "When did you become a Kanaka lover, Boy? This is the last straw! Scullys would turn over in their graves if they realised the man my father encouraged me to marry was turning soft on Hawaiians."

"You're taking your business losses too hard, Atherton, if you ask me," she added suddenly, tears coming into her eyes. It was like the old man's presence had suddenly left her.

She came close and embraced me closely. I kissed her

willingly. It seemed so long since we had made love. I hadn't been feeling up to it since my last business venture failed.

"Believe me, I know how you feel," she said to my astonishment. It was like my wife had two personalities or something.

"It was devastating to me, too, when you lost your position with Michael's firm, and when you failed in these last three ventures. But maybe this time it will be different."

I kissed Jessica again. She responded with some of her long-standing passion and I felt myself become empowered. My libido seemed to be roaring awake from a long slumber.

"Let's go home and make love for the rest of the day," I suggested. "The Plumeria trees are blooming in the solarium and I'll send the servants out on errands."

"Provided you agree we should invest in the hotel Darling," I added. "You know I always come alive when I'm in a risky business venture." All doubts about the investment seemed to disappear from my mind. My body was responding passionately for the first time in months.

"I'll call Theodore in the morning and ask him how much we would need to get in on that hotel hui." I moved Jessica towards the car.

"But what about your poor Hawaiians and their disappearing culture?"

"Forget I ever said those words, Darling. Iwana is probably going senile, anyway. What does he know? Surely what's good for tourism is good for Hawaii and Hawaiians. Besides maybe we can add a little hula in for the tourists at the hotel. That should be enough culture for Iwana."

"You're sounding more like Father all the time. Stop by the liquor store on the way. I want to pick up some Mai Tai ingredients. We'll make love just like the old days. Remember when you first met me, that moonlight swim off the Moana Hotel. Let's do the same tonight. It's a full moon." I snuggled close to Jessica as the chauffeur drove us home.

"I don't want you spending any more time with that old Hawaiian courtier." I nodded in agreement. "I don't think he's a good influence on you at all."

"Whatever you say, Dear," I replied, hoping to reach home before my libido faded again. I'd been worried I'd lost it forever.

Chapter 2.

Investment Gamble.

The next morning I made a call to Theodore Wiltshire. Jessica beamed at me approvingly. I felt like a new man. We had spent the entire night making love.

"All right Atherton, I'll take one final chance on your business sense or lack of it," my dear wife had informed me in the morning. "But fail yet again and I'm going to replace you with someone who is more like my father." I ignored my wife's warning.

"She can't be serious," I thought. "After close to thirty years."

As I picked up the receiver a long-lost pain shot through my belly. I smiled in ecstacy. It was the start of the adrenaline high I used to experience daily running Bridgewater's many enterprises. He had fired me even though I had managed to get the Delegate to Congress to agree to the freeing of twenty-six thousand acres of good sugar land for the planters that should have gone to the Hawaiians with the passage of the Hawaiian Homes Act in 1922.

"It's been too long," I sighed. I felt years lifting off my age as the thought of a new business gamble filled me with energy.

"Aloha, Theodore Wiltshire, please? Atherton Scully, speaking." I shot into the mouthpiece. His secretary put me right through.

"Atherton, I've been trying to reach you for weeks," Wiltshire spoke into the phone with his staccato-like voice. "You're missing out on the investment of a lifetime. I can get you an interest in the new Hotel hui for the Tropical Palace Hotel for one tenth of its actual value."

"That's why I'm calling Theodore. Give me the low-down on the investment will you? Jessica has agreed we should get in on the bottom floor. I've convinced her you've got a winner, there."

"Smart Lady, your wife! Just like her old man, if you ask me. That's one of the reasons I want you in this venture. Rumor has it that your wife's inherited the business know-how of old Damon."

I cringed. "Damn it," I thought. "Jessica has more respect from the business community than I do. Bridgewater must be maligning me all over Honolulu." Irritation revived the doubts I had about the hotel scheme. I tried to find out more about it.

"Look, Theodore, I'm not completely convinced about this deal. What makes you fellows so sure this Hotel is going to be a winner anyway?"

"You wonder about the Tropical Palace Hotel, Atherton. Why it's only blocks away from the most luxurious hotel this side of Los Vegas. And just as nice. Besides you know that new liner, the Malolo. Malolo means flying fish in Hawaiian. That steamer's some flying fish all right. It's cut the distance between Los Angeles and Honolulu by three days."

"What's the Malolo got to do with it?"

"Everything." Wiltshire's voice sounded exasperated. "Why that steamship can transport hundreds of the mainland's elite at a time. Not to mention the rich and famous from Europe, Asia and the Commonwealth. The two main hotels aren't going to be able to handle the volume of reservations."

"So what makes you think the Malolo's passengers are going to stay at the Tropical Palace? The other Waikiki hotels have been capturing the rich crowd all these years. Look how quick the Tropical Palace went into receivership with the stock market crash. Although the other hotels are still carrying on."

Theodore gave a short laugh.

"The Tropical Paradise was under-financed. None of the

Honolulu regulars were on it's Board of Directors. Ask Jessica! She'll tell you how we long-time families run business here in Hawaii. I guess you haven't quite figured it out yet." I winced.

"We've got a contract with the Malolo sewed up. It's with the shipping line that controls the other luxury steamers, too. We take the overflow after the other two hotels. The Board of Directors of the shipping line, which coincidentally I'm on, has given us the exclusive for part of their package deals. Their cruise from San Francisco and Los Angeles now comes with three weeks at either the other hotels or the Tropical Palace. You didn't think we'd leave anything to chance, did you?"

"So what kind of money am I looking at?"

"Don't worry, Atherton. You can afford it. At least Jessica can. The money from old Damon's will alone should cover your contribution. We'll give you a one-fifth interest in the hui for that."

"I don't know if I want to play a long shot if it's going to cost us that much." Anxiety assailed me again. What would become of us if Jessica lost everything she had inherited from her old man.

"Look, I'll tell you what." Wiltshire's voice sounded a little over-eager.

"Maybe I can get the hui to sweeten the pot for you. We're kind of in a bind. We need the balance of the financing now. We've got to get the hotel up and running again completely by the end of next month. The Malolo's owners are putting on a big promotional deal. They intend to send out a boat-load of stock-market crash survivors on a big publicity push. We've got to show the ones that reach our hotel the finest time they've ever had in their lives. First Class all the way."

"What kind of deal are you talking about?"

"Rumor has it you're after a title, not just an investment. How would you like to be the Chairman of the Board of Directors of the Tropical Palace Hotel?"

"Under new management, of course. One of the most

prestigious hotels in all of Hawaii. That way you get to call most of the shots."

I had to admit I was tempted. Bridgewater would be furious when he heard the news.

"You'll announce my appointment in the Sunday Business Section of the paper?"

"Naturally."

"You've got a deal." I repressed my nagging doubts about the tourist industry in Hawaii.

"I'll have the papers drawn up today. Come down to my office on Monday with Jessica and her cheque, certified of course. We've got no time to lose. You've got to take charge of the hotel management fast. They tell me they're a crisis with the Music Director of the hotel, of all things."

"The Music Director? I've heard everything now. Of all things, music is a problem?"

"Yeah, seems the steady clientele is tired of the local talent." Wiltshire filled me in on the problem at hand. He told me that they had been receiving complaints for months about the music. He said that they had a replacement Music Director coming from the Mainland, one of the big band leaders from New York. Wiltshire added that something had to be done about the standard of music in the ballroom. He claimed the Hotel needed to come up with something with more class, something more in line with the latest dance craze on the mainland even if it caused them to deviate from the standard Hawaii fare offered now.

"Don't worry. I'll handle the music crisis." I was ecstatic. The challenge of setting up a hotel in two months seemed to rev up my whole system. I thought furiously.

I told Wiltshire that what the new Music Director needed was some fresh talent. I told him that the group that had been entertaining at the Tropical Palace was stolen from the other hotels years ago and that they had grown stale. I added that big band music was the craze now and that what we needed were younger, new talents. "Don't worry," I advised him. "I'll put an ad in the newspaper today asking for some young blood. You can't expect the tourists to watch the same people forever. Why, some of the local entertainers are from King Kalakaua's time."

"OK, Atherton. We'll trust you to solve this latest crisis and all the others that arise before the Malolo gets here. But just remember it's your responsiblility to impress the pants off our share of the rich and famous when they arrive."

Chapter 3.

Kimi Kai'ika.

My heart swelled up with joy as I spied the answer to my big pilikia, my problem in the Classified Ads.

> "New Polynesian talent wanted for existing luxury hotel under new management in Waikiki. Must be enthusiastic and available in late afternoons and evenings. Substantial salary to the right parties. Audition next Monday, 3:00 p.m. at the Ballroom of the Tropical Palace Hotel."

"If I got one of those jobs I would be able to pay the fees for teacher training after all," I thought, my head reeling with mixed emotions. Triumph had first changed to despair as I had been unexpectedly accepted into teacher training only to realize there was no money to pay the fees. I allowed myself to start to hope again.

"After all, Felice and I have studied the ancient hula nearly all our lives." Resentment at having to go to the demanding hula dance practices that my mother insisted was the duty of our family flooded my mind. She had some weird idea that our 'ohana, our family, had to preserve the old ways. So I was forced to spend three nights a week for all of my Elementary and High School years being driven all the way out to the Makaha Valley to learn ancient hula at the old temple there. None of my friends even knew where I went all the time. The kumu hula teacher kept the location of our hula school secret. We only came out into the open for hula competitions.

I would have rather played with the other kids in Nanakuli instead of dancing ancient hula but maybe it would pay off now.

"Mother always said mastering ancient hula would pay off big, although I don't think she meant it to pay off financially," I warned myself."

"You see, Kimi," Mother always said. "You help preserve old ways. Your Father be proud if he still live. Ancient Hula Kahiko make all 'ohana proud. You see."

I reached for the phone. I could still hear the voice of Mrs. Nakamura, the teacher at the Ilawu School ringing in my ears as she congratulated Felice and me.

"Kimi Kai`ika and Felice Santos, you have made me so proud. You're the first of my Kanaka and Portuguese students to pass the Standard English exam that allows you to enter the Territorial Normal School and become teachers."

"We've passed, Mrs. Nakamura?" I'd cried out in astonishment. The Standard English exam had been incredibly hard. My Hawaiian and Portuguese friends all spoke pidgin instead of standard English. It was sort of a protest against westerners and all their put downs towards both Native Hawaiians and the other people that had come to Hawaii to work the plantations. As a result I had to concentrate really hard to use standard English grammar in my written work. I had also had to use every available minute of the time allotted to pore over the multiple choice reading questions on the exam and search deep within myself to come up with answers for the essay questions.

"Explain exactly what it means to be independent," had been the topic of the main essay. I'd had no end of trouble trying to write that one. Native Hawaiians valued family affiliation over independent achievement but I sensed that the non-Hawaiian judges wouldn't like that approach. But it was all right. I could stop blaming myself now for not studying harder. I had passed, after all.

"Yes, Kimi. Take a look at the list of those who passed." Mrs. Nakamura went to the front of the class.

"See students. It can be done, Kimi and Felice have passed the Standard English exam that let's you go on to College level or the Territorial Normal School. Now, if the rest of you would only give up speaking that horrible pidgin you insist on speaking all the time and work harder you could become someone of importance, too."

"Why most of you Kanakas don't even pass the Standard English exam that allows you to go on to Grade Eight. Most of you are on Vocational Tracks I and II as a result. We have to put some of you in the work stream even before you are nine and ten."

The class had groaned.

"Auwe, Mrs. Nakamura, you wan us be stuck-up or somethin? Our parents say we need be free Kanakas. Grow taro, fish mahi-mahi, gather limu. Surf big ones off Haleiwa, Waimea Bay."

"You would rather become workers for the plantations, students?" Mrs. Nakamura said in horror. "Rather than school teachers like Kimi and Felice? That's what Vocation Tracks I and II lead you to, you know. Why, I thought you students wanted to be city people. Or do you really want to become rural plantation labor?"

"No way wan be teachers, Mrs. Nakamura. We wan be Beach Boys, crazy surfers, like Duke. He show way for Kanakas."

"Duke!" Mrs. Nakamura said increduously.

"Duke Kahanamoku. You know Duke. Win gold medals, swimming at Olympics. Now Sheriff of Waikiki."

"Stop that, class! That's just what I'm talking about. How many Duke Kahanamoku's can there be? You live in a dream world. None of you have even one ounce of ambition. What Kimi and Felice have done is a truly wonderful accomplishment."

Then it had struck me.

"But there's no money for school fees, Mrs. Nakamura," I'd blurted. "Tutu says I have to go work in the laundry like she does, or my brother Kimo will have to leave school. Our landlord has doubled our rent again."

"You Kanakas!" My heart had frozen when Mrs. Nakamura looked at me with a look of such contempt. Her voice was filled with sarcasm.

"No wonder you Kanakas are always at the bottom of the heap. You mean, Kimi, that even when you get such a splendid opportunity as being accepted into the Territorial Normal School you have no motivation to persevere. Why can't you be more like the Japanese students on Oahu. Why, every one of them has passed the Standard English Exam. My Japanese students and their families see to it that they make something of their lives."

"But Mrs. Nakamura," I'd protested. "My family isn't from the royalty. We have no money from sale of lands or Government jobs. My father was killed in a storm fishing off of Nanakuli. My mother supports us by selling leis when the steamship comes in at the Aloha Tower. As hard as Tutu and Mother work there's no money left for Territorial Normal School fees."

"Kimi Kai`ika, don't be so apathetic. All you Hawaiians want is sympathy and handouts. What kind of job is lei making?"

I blanched. My mother's leis were famous amongst our people for their color, creativity and beauty. Hawaiians came from all over Oahu to buy her leis on special occasions, like luaus for weddings or births.

"Mrs. Nakamura has no understanding of what my 'ohana thinks is important," I realised.

"You think my family had money?" Mrs. Nakamura continued, her voice filled with sarcasm. But I knew I was not supposed to say anything. My Tutu's orders when I went to the city school came into my mind.

"No argue with teacher, Kimi. No look teacher in eyes, not polite. Keep family matters secret."

I lowered my gaze. I tried to follow Tutu's orders. But the class were all staring at me. The Japanese students were jeering at the Hawaiians and my friends were all set to defend me.

"Don worry, Kimi. We geev em da stink eye," my friend Keolo said.

"Shame flooded me. My face went beet red. I was the cause of the fight in the classroom. Then I felt myself getting angry at the things Mrs. Nakamura was saying about Hawaiians.

'Why, Kimi," she continued. "My father was one of the four hundred thousand plantation workers brought here to work the sugar-cane fields? And he put me and all my brothers and sisters through school. How do you think I became a teacher?"

Then it happened. I snapped. I lost my temper. I couldn't stop myself. I was so hurt and angry at her attack on my family. I violated Tutu's orders.

"But at least your father could find work, Mrs. Nakamura," I pointed out. "And you had a place to stay and could grow your own vegetables and raise chickens. All my family could do after my father's death was gather limu at the seashore. We had to move to the city. There was nothing for us in Nanakuli after my father's death. We couldn't even pay our rent."

"Nonsense, Kimi. Remember, I know your family. If your mother hadn't thrown money to the wind buying your brother ukeleles and surf-boards, and having you driven to hula classes in Waianae, funds would have been available for your courses today."

"Kimo has a special talent for music and surfing," Mrs. Nakamura," I'd protested. "And dancing Hula Kahiko is sacred to the Gods. At least that's what my Kumu Hula, Aunt Auhea, says."

"Sacred? That unmelodious chanting? Why, I bet the Gods, if they are listening, are covering their ears." The Japanese members of the class laughed."

"Mrs. Nakamura. Our hula halau has won the hula Kahiko competition on Oahu for five years in a row. And Kimo won the long board competition at Makaha last summer." I suddenly realised I was shouting.

Tears came into my eyes at Mrs. Nakamura's words about the hula. I realised she would never understand. I bolted out the door. I managed to make it out of the school grounds before I broke down into complete sobs. Tutu understood when I had told her about passing the exam, and needing money for the fees, just like she understands everything. I didn't dare tell her about what Mrs. Nakamura had said about our family.

"No worry, Kimi," she said, cuddling me close. "Tutu know wat mean fo you become teacher. My mother, she dead, but always say wan you really need somethin dere be way. I go talk Mano." I realised Tutu was talking about our family ancestor god, the shark God, Mano.

"I go fo limu tomorrow, Kimi. Maybe Mano find way fo you going dat school."

"And now this newspaper advertisement," I thought. "Right after Tutu talked to Mano in the old way. Why, the Tropical Palace Hotel is located on the bus line to the Territorial Normal School. I could go directly from the school to the Hotel for the afternoon and evening shows."

"Tutu," I yelled. "Tutu, I've found a way to get the money for Kimo's school fees and for Territorial Normal School. I showed her the newspaper ad."

"Mother no like, Kimi. She train you in hula Kahiko. Tink our family have sacred duty carry on old ways. I no tink so. It my husband who chant fo King Kalakaua court. Husband say must preserve old ways. He devote life but I tink maybe waste. But your mother, she believe, pay have you learn Hula Kahiko."

"Then wouldn't mother be happy to see the Hula Kahiko danced before the tourists?" I argued. "Why would she object, Tutu, if it meant I could go to Normal School."

"You no understan, Kimi. Hula Kahiko sacred. Haoles no understand Kanakas ways. 'Ohanas no tell Haoles chants from past. My husband, your mother and your father hate Haole ways.

Live away Haole world. Tutu not want country. Like City. Stay Honolulu. But your parents take old path. Until Father killed. Mother not able afford rent, Nanakuli. She force live wit Tutu in City. But hope someday go back where only Kanakas live. Mother say maybe go Waipio Valley on Big Island."

"Tutu, I don't want to go to some desolate valley where no one lives. I want to be a teacher in Honolulu."

"Tutu know, Kimi. You mo like Tutu dan mother or Grandfather. But you study Hula Kahiko, sacred hula, Kimi, suppose connect wit Hawaiian gods. Mother be sad if dance fo tourists. Give way secrets. Haoles no understand Hula Kahiko. They no like. No Aloha inside, like us."

"But if it way get you teacher school?" Tutu seemed to go into deep thought.

"Maybe no tell Mother bout ad, Kimi. Tutu say you go Honolulu fo groceries. See wat happen."

"Thanks Tutu," I sobbed. "You always understand everything." My head ached. I didn't think I would ever understood why my mother kept us from many of the normal activities kids did in Honolulu. She forbid us to have Haole friends and both my brother Kimo and myself were forced to spend almost all our free time doing things my mother said were important to the people of old.

"That's one of the reasons I wanted to become a teacher," I realised. At least I would be allowed to stay in the City. I was terrified that if I didn't go to Territorial Normal School I would have to go to Waipio Valley to grow taro like mother was always threatening.

"How does Mother know Haoles didn't like Hula Kahiko," I asked myself. "Maybe Felice and I could dance it at the Hotel and surprise Mother with it being applauded. How would we know if we didn't try?" I rationalised.

Chapter 4.

Teri'i And Ito.

"Ito, Brah, maybee dis answer to beeg problem." Teri'i Fa'atua poked his rather plump Japanese friend and handed him the ad from the Honolulu newspaper.

"I no read but tink picture say hotel need Polynesian talent. Where mo Polynesian talent dan us?" Teri'i's friend put down his prize possession, his ukelele, and read the ad with intense concentration.

"You right, Teri'i-san. That's what this ad says." Ito jumped out of his usual lethargic, ukelele-playing self and started to throw clothes frantically into a suitcase.

"Pack, Teri'i-san," he ordered. "We've got to go to Lihue right away. The steamer comes into Nawiliwili harbor tomorrow. We've just about got enough time to make it if we leave immediately."

"But Plantation fire if go Ito. You know. Luna never geev time off in middle week."

"No choice, Teri'i-san. Might be chance of a lifetime. How often does a hotel change management in Waikiki. Why, maybe they are getting rid of their old entertainers. We're just what they are looking for. They do say 'Polynesian talent,' don't they?" Ito grabbed the paper again.

"But Ito-san?" Teri'i stood up in front of him, blocking his way with his six-foot-four bulk. Muscles bulged everywhere thanks to lifting sugar-cane twelve hours a day for months on end.

"Where we leev?" he worried. "Plantation fire if go Honolulu middle week. No where leev if hotel no want us. Teri'i not able go back Tahiti now if no get job. Brudder write, French taking over family acreages. Mudder lose land. All business people, Tahiti, not Tahitians. Say land title acreage no good fo many Tahitians. Sell to French. Build hotel. Brudder say nutting can be done, put in jail if protest."

"We can stay with my family, Teri'i-san. Father-san will be glad Ito-san is coming back to Honolulu. I'll tell him I'll enroll in the University of Hawaii business program like he wants me to. He'll even let you stay with us if he thinks I've changed my mind and given up on becoming a ukelele player. You have no idea how upset father-san was when I told him that I didn't want to go into his business."

"Dat how you wound up Makee Plantation, Ito-san?"

"Father-san kick Ito out of house, Teri'i, when I told him I was going to become a ukelele player. But he will let us come back if he thinks I've relented."

"You lie Father, Ito?"

"No, Teri'i-san. I really will enroll for the business degree if the Hotel hires us. I imagine I can fit the classes around the entertainment times anyway. Believe me, Ito-san has had enough of plantation labor."

"You go University, Ito? Dey let you in University?"

"Teri'i-san! Ito Nimura one smart Samarai. Just like the rest of my family. I've got straight "A" marks from my High School. But I would rather play the ukelele than become a businessman like my father. I love show business. Just like you do."

"Teri'i understand, Ito. Any spare time practice Tamure dance, sword-swallow and fire-dance learn from Polynesian dance troupes Kauai. Anyting better dan load sugar-cane fo dollar day."

"But what bout paycheck. Luna no geev til Friday. Teri'i no

money fo steamer. And tink Teri'i owe mo dan make dis week at company store."

"Don't worry. Ito-san will get you to Honolulu. He pulled out a roll of bills from his pocket.

"Where you get money, Ito-san?"

"From mother-san. Mother-san Okinawan, not Japanese. She understands you have to be true to what's in your heart. Her family was not happy that she married a Japanese man. She understands why I don't want to follow in father-san's footsteps. She understands I want to be a ukelele player in my heart. Mother-san secretly sends me money."

"Why Japanese, Okinawans, not get along, Ito-san?"

"I don't know. Something to do with history, I guess. But let's get out of here, right now. Before anyone realises what we're doing. Maybe we can get a ride to Nawiliwili Harbor in that delivery truck that's about to leave from the company store." Ito looked out the poor excuse for a window, a plastic sheet you could barely peer through.

"The truck's still there. Let's go."

"Wat I do wit clothes, Ito? And fire dance stuff?" "Use this." Ito threw a huge duffle bag at Teri'i. Ito packed musical instruments and clothes into several more of the large bags.

"You go Nawiliwili Harbor?" Teri'i ask truck driver.

"Dey know you goin?" the large Filipino fellow queried, pointing towards the luna's shack.

"Sure, Brah," Ito said handing him bill from his pocket. The driver grinned.

"You go Lihue?" Teri'i asked again. "I trow bags back truck?"

"Sure Brah. Filipe ask no questions fo sure." Ito handed him another bill."

"Maybee beeg break fo us Ito-san?"

"You bet it is!"

Chapter 5.

Music Director In Paradise.

"What a break!" Winston Emory told himself as he mused over his unexpected fate. He was seated drinking a tropical concoction in the luxurious ballroom of the Tropical Palace Hotel in Waikiki. He stared at the opulent crystal chandeliers in approval.

"This ballroom is as impressive as any hotel in New York," I thought. A light breeze was blowing in from the open lanai and the smell of Plumeria was everywhere.

"Here, I'd thought I'd hit the bottom of the bucket after I had to disband my orchestra for lack of engagements. And now, just because some big-wig from Hawaii heard me during that last week in New York I get to be the Music Director in Paradise."

I stood up as a fellow who looked somewhat of an older version of himself, good looking, tall and lean, made his way over to the table. I suspected from the fellow's expensive tuxedo and greying hair that he might be my new boss.

"I take it you're Winston Emory, my new Music Director," the man confirmed my hunch. He stood up and I shook his hand. The man's handshake was firm and business-like.

"You must be Mr. Atherton Scully, the Chairman of the Board of this hotel?" I ventured.

"Welcome to Hawaii, Emory." Scully's voice suited him. It

was gruff and brisk and suited to his business-like manner. He got right to the point.

"Ordinarily, my wife Jessica and I would show you around Oahu but I'll be frank. You've got a little more than a month to pull together a full musical medley that will impress the pants off part of a boatload of stock market crash survivors. They're coming to Honolulu on a special charter of the luxury liner, Malolo."

I could sense Scully's anxiety.

"This is really important to him," I could tell.

"The success of this hotel depends on the impression you're going to make on those charter passengers, Emory. I'm depending on you to impress those guests big-time."

"Any suggestions as to how I'm to do that, Atherton?" I tried to appear ten times as confident as I really was.

"What the Hell do I really know about Hawaiian music?" was what I was really thinking to myself.

"Call me Mr. Scully, Emory." Any self-confidence I had left evaporated. "Great," I thought. "I sure started out on the right foot with him."

"Music's not my game, Emory. That's why the Board of Directors hired you. But I can tell you that you've got to score big with a sophisticated, international crowd used to spending time in luxurious world resorts. How you do it is up to you."

"Any idea why I was selected for this job, Mr. Scully?" I was hoping for any kind of clue as to what whoever hired me liked about my music.

"Yeah. Seems one of the main cash suppliers besides myself for the hui that controls this hotel, a fellow by the name of Norman Baker, heard your group in New York. Thought some number with a sophisticated rhythm to it was the 'Cat's Meow,' I understand. He want's you to do the same kind of thing here. The tired-old hulas and the beach-boy songs just aren't making it anymore."

"Mind if I contact Mr. Baker, Sir? Maybe he can tell me which arrangement he was impressed with?"

"No way, Emory. Believe me, leave any interaction with Norman Baker to me. He's on the Board of every major Company on Oahu. Norman's hasn't got the time to chat with you about his favorite music pieces."

"It must have been the Latin American number I included in my repertoire the last week of our New York run." I thought. It was the talk of the town. I felt trapped. "I don't think I even brought the music for that with me," was all I could think. "And I did finish with an Hawaiian number—'Aloha Oe,' but that's hardly got rhythm to it, that old piece. It was written in the late 1800's by some Hawaiian Queen, I think."

"Tell you something, though, Emory. That fellow Baker has some kind of bee in his bonnet. Thinks Hawaii has a special role to play in the Western Hemisphere or something. Seems to think that these little Islands are the bridge between East and West or something like that. All I know is that Norman Baker doesn't want our Hotel orchestra to come out sounding like the little hick band that's it's been sounding like for too long."

"Then what you're looking for is a major musical reorganization?"

"That's right. I'll give you a free hand to accomplish the reorganization any way you can. I've even put in an ad for new blood in the newspaper. I've got auditions set up for you, starting today at 3.00 p.m. But believe me, either Norman Baker and our wealthy clientele on the Malolo get something that makes them think Hawaii is First Class or you get a ticket along with them back to New York."

"I understand. I'll do my best."

"We're in this together, young man. I need a High Class sound that has something to do with Hawaii and I understand you need money to pay some of your debts off from your stock market losses. Believe me, the success of this hotel means everything to my wife and me."

He reached for my right hand. I tried to make my handshake feel a lot more substantial than the state of my present knowledge of Hawaiian music. It was in about the same condition as my bank account, pretty well non-existent.

"Maybe he'll settle for a Hollywood chorus line with a few Hawaiian words thrown in," I thought desperately. "No, that will never do. Bridging the gap between East and West. Sounds ambitious. I'll have to think about that for awhile. That has possibilities. It sounds like a major Hollywood plot line. Maybe something in the stage-show line. My mind began to fill with possible approaches.

"We would need a more powerful orchestra than what's here now," I realised. I looked at the few musicians at the bar strumming ukeleles. Perhaps if I added violins or maybe brass?"

"See you at 3:00 p.m. then?" Scully went back to other pressing matters. A horde of hotel staff descended on him as soon as he left the entrance to the Ballroom.

I prayed desperately. "Inspiration, I need inspiration," I thought. "But how am I going to put together an entire evening's worth of High-class Hawaiian music in such a short time?"

"Maybe the auditions will give me some idea of what Hawaiian music is like?" I thought. "Surely there must be sheet music somewhere. Scores written down. What the Hell have they been doing in these hotels since they opened?"

"Hey waiter, bring me another of those tropical concoctions, will you?" By the time the auditions started I was feeling much better. The alcohol had convinced me there would be no problem putting something together. I'd done it so many time in the past. I stared at the line-up of would-be performers forming down the hallway.

Atherton Scully came back at 3:00 just like he'd said. On his arm was a well-endowed, mature woman with flaming red hair and steely blue eyes. She was dripping with expensive jewelry.

"Allow me to introduce my wife, Jessica, Emory. Darling, this is Winston Emory, our new Music Director."

"Honored to meed you Mrs. Scully." I bowed and grasped the lady's hand in mine, giving it a kiss.

"Call me Jessica, Winston," she replied in a senuous, throaty voice. I appreciated the lady's considerable sex appeal.

"Bet she was some bomb-shell when she was younger," I thought. "Still is, I suppose, given the right circumstances like dim light and the right amount of alcohol. I bet Scully has his hands full with a lady like that," I surmised.

"Ready to start the auditions?" Scully asked pointedly.

"Send in the first applicant," I directed the Maitre D confidently. Immediately some tall, Hawaiian guy in his mid forties and his guitar went up to the mike set up in the ballroom. He sang three verses and my feeling of well-being immediately evaporated.

"Yacky Hula Hickey Dula," sang the fellow in an off-key falsetto. Guests in the audience laughed appreciatively but I winced painfully. The piece was awful. I recognised the tune as an 1916 Al Jolson hit.

"My God, I sighed audibly to the Scully's. "Isn't that melody, 'Aloha Oe', played backwards." I was sure it was. I glanced over at Jessica Scully. She had a deep scowl on her face.

Despite my despair I tried to joke the audition off.

"I wonder how the Malolo's passengers would like that one?" I chuckled.

"My father, Damon Scully, would have had that performer exiled to the mainland," Scully's wife barked. I could tell she had no sense of humor at all.

"Thanks very much," I mercifully silenced the performer as he started another strange number called, "Oh, How She Could Yacki Hacki Wicky Wacky Woo."

"Please give your name and phone number to the Maitre D. The Hotel will be in touch as soon as we decide." Atherton Scully looked relieved.

"Wouldn't you like to hear 'They're Wearing 'Em Higher in Hawaii?'" he questioned.

"Tomorrow," I silenced him. "Tomorrow morning, 9:00 sharp, same place!" I sensed the interview process was going to take longer than Scully had thought.

"Perhaps those two hula dancers?" I suggested to the Maitre D. The girls looked so innocent, hopeful and young. "Surely they won't do something from another time era?" I thought.

"Oh, no," I muttered. An ancient Hawaiian lady was coming up to the stage with the two young, exotic-looking and beautiful girls weighed down with an overgrown gourd of some kind.

"Wouldn't you young ladies like the hotel musicians to play for you," I suggested plaintively. I could see Jessica Scully's scowl deepening as she stared at the old crone.

"Kahiko not use Haole instruments," the old lady glared at me. I sat down and braced myself. "That must be the old crone's name." I thought, 'Kahiko.' The old woman started chanting in Hawaiian and striking the gourd in a rhythm I'd never heard before. I found the performance distinctly painful. It lacked any semblance of western-style harmony. The two girls moved onto the stage and did a hula to the rhythm of the gourd.

"Well, at least they would have some hope of arousing the libido of wealthy stock-brokers," I thought. I appreciated the girl's physical beauty. "Maybe if we put them in scanty costumes?" I thought. "Coconut cups should do it and grass skirts."

I endured the old lady's chanting for as long as I could. I glanced at Jessica Scully. She was looking outright angry now.

"My father never could stand that ghastly chanting," she commented. "He always said the Kanakas were worshiping idols."

I jumped up and ended the performance.

"Thanks, Kahiko," I addressed the old woman, effectively stopping the performance. I wondered why everyone in the ballroom tittered. The young ladies looked completely crushed.

"Make sure you give your names and phone numbers to our Maitre D," I whispered to the girls as the old crone stalked haughtily off the stage.

"I want you back here tomorrow morning at nine o'clock for another rehearsal. But without Kahiko," I whispered confidentially to the most Hawaiian-looking of the two girls. A faint smile transformed her features. "She's really beautiful," I decided. "Even if I do have to put some western rhythm into that hula myself. I motioned them towards the Maitre D.

"I want them back tomorrow without the old crone for another audition," I told the Scully's. "Maybe we can get them to change their style to something more westernised?" Atherton Scully nodded understandingly.

Two fellows dressed in western clothes carrying guitars were next. Their Hawaiian falsetto blended well but I couldn't understand a word they were saying. Whatever they were singing sounded like it belonged at a Sunday church service.

"What the Hell kind of music is that?" I asked Atherton Scully. I was getting really worried about my ignorance of Hawaiian music.

"Himeni," Jessica Scully answered. It's Hawaiian-style church music. Himeni is patterned after music composed by the Reverend Lorenzo Lyons, an early missionary on the Big Island. Father said that the Kanakas liked Reverend Lyons' music so well they stole the hymn books from every church on the Island. After that they never did another productive thing. Just played and sang their lives away."

The guitarists ended their number. They started another but this time some of the words were in English and they seemed to be singing about romance. "Adios ke aloha," I made out.

"What kind of music is that?" I asked the Scully's.

"Secular himeni," Jessica announced. "The old Hawaiian royalty were fond of composing music like that. My father used to say that if the ali`i had spent as much time thinking about business as they had composing music it might have not been necessary to depose them."

The musicians finished their number and the house audience clapped appreciatively. Then the two musicians began to adjust the strings on their guitars. I started as they began to sing in Hawaiian again.

"The guitars sound completely different somehow," I remarked to the Scully's.

"Yeah," Scully sounded gruff. "It's called slack-key guitar. I understand each slack-key artist has his own unique way of tuning his strings."

"Father said that the Spanish cowboys brought over to the Islands left their guitars behind when they left. But they hadn't left them tuned. Kanakas experimented and came up with different ways of tuning them."

"The sound is great," I acknowledged. "Maybe if we could get them to sing in English?"

"Good luck," Atherton Scully replied. "Our former Music Director tried for years without success."

"This isn't going to be easy, is it?"

"I've got full confidence in you, My Boy. Scully replied. I motioned to the Maitre D.

"Get those fellow's names," I requested. "Won't you join me in some liquid refreshment I asked the Scully's. Perhaps one of these tropical concoctions I'm drinking?".

"You mean Zombies," Jessica looked displeased.

No wonder my head is starting to pound, I realised." The Scully's ordered champagne. I ordered beer. Beer often brought me down painlessly from an alcohol-induced high.

"Now what?" I thought as a short, chubby, Japanese looking fellow little more than a kid moved to the mike. He was wearing dark-rimmed spectacles and he was carrying a short stringed instrument I'd never seen before. I noticed Jessica Scully groan.

The Japanese boy motioned to a troupe of hula maidens standing hopefully in the hallway. The maidens, dresses in long outfits came in and formed a line in front of us.

"How come those beautiful young things are dressed in gowns up to their necks?" I asked.

"A lot of the present day hula dates from King Kalakaua's time," Jessica Scully replied. "Victorian dresses were all in style then."

The Japanese fellow put his instrument to his lips and carressed it with his tongue.

I cringed as the kid produced sounds using his lips, mouth and teeth that somehow resembled the rhythm chanting done by the old crone. The hula maidens dance was the same kind of unwestern rhythm that I'd found so disconcerting earlier.

"What kind of instrument is that?" I asked the Scullys.

"Another of those dreadful pagan instruments the Kanaka's used before the missionaries mercifully put a stop to their dances," Jessica replied. "I believe this one is called a Ukeke."

Seeing her irritation I stopped the performance. The hula maidens filed off.

"Ito," one of the hotel musicians shouted to the Japanese kid.

"Show them what you can do with the ukelele, Brah." He passed his ukelele to the kid.

Ito adjusted the instrument and then strummed it rhymically. To my complete surprise he broke into a Hawaiian version of the jazz and blues popular on the mainland.

"What's that?" I asked the Scully's.

"Aloha Means I Love You," Atherton Scully, replied. "It's a new song that's rather popular with the tourists," he added.

I whistled as the rhythm of the piece intensified. The Japanese kid had talent all right.

"Play another one, Ito," I requested. The young fellow called the over-dressed, hula girls back. They formed a line on the stage again.

"My Hawaiian Tomboy," the Japanese kid sang and played. The hula maidens dutifully did a hula that portrayed tomboy-like activities in Honolulu. The audience laughed uproariously. Even Jessica Scully managed a smile.

"What's your last name, Ito?" I queried as the laughter in the ballroom to the comic hula died down.

"Ito Nimura," he replied.

"Come back at 9:00 tomorrow," I directed. "And make sure you bring those hula maidens with you. But find some grass skirts for them, will you?"

"Thank you, Emory-San," the young kid looked immensely relieved.

"I'll make sure he plays a ukelele not a ukeke," I promised Jessica Scully.

A handsome blonde-haired Caucasian guy stepped up to the mike next. He seemed to know the hotel musicians.

"The usual," he directed them. The musicians played the opening strands for 'Danny Boy.' As soon as the fellow opened his mouth I knew my luck was looking up. He had a powerful Irish tenor that reached every nook and cranny of the ballroom. Jessica Scully beamed.

"That's Norman Baker's favorite tenor," she told her husband.

"Beautiful," I responded as the audience applause died down.

"Tell him he's hired," I directed the Maitre D. Have him report at 9:00 a.m. tomorrow. I'd like to find out what's in his repertoire."

"Good work, Winston." Jessica looked pleased. "That's Alan Costairs, my favorite tenor. He sings a lot with the Royal Hawaiian Band. I told him about this audition."

"I'll create some songs for him in our new musical medley." I promised. I felt my confidence returning.

"How about a romance theme, Jessica. Prince Kane meets his Princess, or something like that."

"Wonderful, Winston. Norman Baker told me you'd be perfect for the job. I'm beginning to see why."

Next a young Polynesian fellow looking like he was going to audition for Mr. America came up on the stage. His strong body was loaded with muscles. I looked at his face and realised he had the craggy good looks that drove females wild. The young man was dressed in a revealing Polynesian costume and he carried two flaming batons in his hands.

The women in the audience sighed in appreciation as he assumed a provocative posture. The hotel musicians broke into a fast-moving rhythm and the fellow went through a series of sexual gyrations, acrobatically juggling the flaming torches.

"What's that?" I asked the Scully's, admiration evident in my voice.

"Samoan fire-dancing," Jessica Scully answered. "It's all the rage on Kauai, right now."

The fire-dancer finished his hazardous-looking dance and then went into a sword-swallowing routine. The ladies in the audience gasped in horror as a two-foot sword disappeared down the fellow's throat.

"Good-going, Teri'i-san," I could hear the young, Japanese, ukelele player encouraging the sword-swallower.

"I guess they must be partners," I decided.

"What do you think?" I asked Jessica Scully.

"I don't think much of the sword swallowing," she remarked. "But the Samoan fire dancing is quite invigorating."

"Tell that fire dancer he's hired," I said to the Maitre D. Have him come back at 9:00 tomorrow, too."

Chapter 6.

Compromise.

"Felice, we've got to go back to the Tropical Palace Hotel tomorrow morning like the Music Director said. How else are we going to pay for Normal School?"

"Kimi, don't be a fool. You saw how that Music Director and the audience reacted to our hula. Your mother is right. Tourists don't appreciate the Hula Kahiko. And that Emory guy calling our kumu hula 'Kahiko.' Auntie Auhea nearly died with embarrassment."

"I know, Felice. I couldn't believe their reaction but if you think about it maybe it's time we danced something besides the Hula Kahiko. We need the money those jobs will bring us to attend Normal School. Otherwise we're going to spend the rest of our lives working in a laundry or a pineapple cannery for a pittance."

All of a sudden anger flooded my mind. Bitter anger surged at all the years I had spent doing what my mother wanted and not being able to do what I'd wanted.

"No wonder the people at the Hotel didn't like the Hula Kahiko, Felice. It's so different from the music we hear on the radio nowadays. Who wants to listen to or look at something from another Century?"

"Your mother and Aunt Auhea would call you a kipi, Kimi, a traitor, if they heard you say that. A traitor to your culture."

A strange mixture of emotions choked me at Felice's words. My face turned red. I felt a totally upsetting mixture of emotions surge through me. Guilt and shame merged with anger and pain.

"Felice, there must be some way we can both be true to our culture and escape from poverty," I choked. "Maybe we could dance the newer hulas now and then add some of the Hula Kahiko later."

"What do you mean, Kimi, newer hulas?"

"Hula like the other hula troups do. You know, hula with accompaniment of the ukelele and guitars. The tourists like that."

"Kimi, our kumu hula and our parents are going to disown us if we do that. Auntie Auhea says that Music Director is just after our bodies. You know she's ordered us to ignore that 9:00 appointment. She never told our parents about the audition this time because she promised your grandmother she wouldn't. But can you imagine what she'll do if she finds out we went back to the Tropical Palace Hotel again. And if she finds out we danced hula other than the Hula Kahiko. Imagine how mad your mother will be if she finds out."

"Look Felice, maybe Mother doesn't have to find out about this." I felt a strange surge of craftiness fill my mind. "Somehow I've got to convince Felice we must go to that audition," I thought. "Or I'm going to wind up in some desolate valley growing taro for the rest of my life."

"Do you really want me to work in a laundry for the rest of my life? Or do you want me to wind up in the Waipio Valley growing taro? I think I'd rather die. And what about you? Are you going to marry that older Plantation worker your father wants you to become engaged to? Just because he comes from the same village in Portugal your father comes from. Why he's at least twice your age."

I knew that would make Felice think twice. She hated that guy.

"Don't even say such a thing, Kimi. You make me shudder."

"Then think of a dance we can do tomorrow that'll get the

Music Director to hire us. We've got to stop doing things just because our parents tell us to do them."

"Kimi, it's already 8:00 at night. The Catholic Church youth group I'm supposed to be at is getting out now. I've got to go home. If my father finds out I lied so I could meet with you I'm going to be grounded for life. Besides, what am I going to tell my parents tomorrow? What reason can I give for going to Honolulu so soon again?"

"Tell your parents we're working part-time in the laundry with Tutu, Felice. I'll talk to her. I know she'll cover for us."

"Your Tutu us so understanding, Kimi. If only Portuguese parents were more like Hawaiian ones."

"My mother isn't going to understand. But I'm not going to let anyone get in my way from earning enough money for those school fees. It's our whole lives that are at stake, I know it."

"I'll met you at the Hotel at 8:00 but I don't know what good it's going to do. What are we going to do at that rehearsal? We don't even have anyone to accompany us."

"The Hotel musicians will, Felice. If we can think of a dance we can do that they play all the time. Don't worry, I'll think of something."

Back at the Tropical Palace Hotel Ballroom auditions were finally coming to an end. Atherton Scully had stayed for the entire audition. His wife had left partway through with a disapproving scowl on her face.

"Don't look so disappointed Emery," Scully tried to cheer me up.

"Thanks Mr. Scully," I uttered as he ordered some much needed food. I hoped my inner terror wasn't showing through. I was about to throw in the towel. I had never seen so much variety in Regional music before. It didn't seem to be anchored by a common theme at all. We had experienced everything from a dancing monkey doing the hula to a miniature flute ensemble playing Mozart.

"What have I got out of that?" I checked my list.

"One Irish tenor with an operetta style, two young and gorgeous hula girls, if they can be persuaded to let me re-choreograph them, three itinerant violin players that play Verdi, two slack-key guitar artists, if I can convince them to sing more in English, a talented Japanese ukelele player, and a guy who says he's a Prince from Tahiti that can jump over flaming torches and swallow a foot of live flame."

"Then there are the minstrels playing 'Waikiki Mermaid' in ragtime and the tuba group playing what sounds like Prussian marches from the 19th. Century. What kind of music revue can I build out of that?" I despaired.

"It's a start, Emory," my boss repeated. "But remember that we don't have a great deal of time left. Look maybe if you were more specific about what kind of talent you want. Leave me a note specifying exactly what additional talent you need and I'll put another ad in the newspaper tomorrow."

"Mr. Scully, I've got to get my hands on some authentic, old, Hawaiian sheet music. I've got to make the new revue look like it comes from somewhere, like out of the Hawaiian past at least. Is there a music studio in Honolulu I can buy it from or a music library?"

"There is some sheet music around, Emory. but unfortunately most of the stuff has been written by mainland people. Like 'Hawaiian Bluebird,' and 'Honolulu, America Loves You,' but I don't imagine that's what you have in mind. What time era are you referring to?"

"Pre-contact Hawaii. You know, before the Europeans came."

"You've got quite a problem, there, Emory. The authentic Hawaiian music from long ago wasn't written down. Hawaiians come from an oral tradition not a written one. I believe Henry Berger, the fellow King Kamehameha V brought over from Prussia to Europeanize Hawaiian music, recorded some of the old tunes but he never published them. Some of the old stuff was passed on by ear by certain Hawaiian families. But those families jealously guard their repertoires, passing them on only to members of their own family."

I groaned.

"I think there's some academic over in the Bishop Museum that's recording some of the old stuff. She's been taking live recordings from old Hawaiians in all the rural areas since 1926. Says she's saving the music for posterity. But I've heard some of the recordings. They sound just like the Hula Kahiko, the one that your two charming, hula girls were dancing with the old crone chanting."

"You mean Kahiko wasn't the old woman's name. No wonder everyone in the Ballroom burst into laughter."

"Don't worry about it, Emory. It's not the local people you have to impress. It's our visitors."

"The harmony in that chanting is not pleasing to western ears, Mr. Scully. Your wealthy stockbrokers won't like it."

"I know Emory. We couldn't agree more."

"But the type of music revue upper class western people appreciate involve medleys anchored in an historical tradition. I jazz up the old songs, give them rhythm that can be danced to and some historical cover."

"I can see what you're getting at Emory. Look, Jessica has quite a lot of contacts with the local orchestra and our opera group. I'll pass on your problem to her. Maybe she knows someone who can play some of the old pieces for you."

"Thanks Mr. Scully. I'll have the wording for the newspaper ads for you shortly."

The next morning I went for a quick swim in the sparkling surf. It seemed to lessen the pounding headache I'd gotten up with. I felt rejuvenated. I went over to the Tropical Palace determined to make something wonderful out of the motley group of entertainers lined up outside the ballroom.

"Aloha Mr. Emory," the hopefuls all yelled as I went into the bar.

"Hair of the dog?" the bartender eyed me knowingly.

"God no," I complained. "Just a whiskey and chaser. Those Zombies you supplied me with last night didn't agree too well."

"It's not the liquor, it's the mixer that causes the trouble."

I moved behind a potted palm in the bar and surveyed my group of hopefuls. The Tahitian fire and sword dancer and the Japanese ukelele player were deep in conversation with the two young hula maidens I had asked to return for auditions.

"Not young love, I hope," I thought. "I'll never get this revue together if they start seeing stars in each others eyes." I moved closer to hear their conversation.

"Are you truly a Prince from Tahiti?" the younger of two hula girls questioned my flame-swallower.

"Kimi Kai`ika," I recalled the kid's name. "I like that. She's very good looking and she's obviously been well trained at dancing, too. Maybe I can make her into a star," I allowed myself to hope.

"Kimi, Teri'i force make confession," the flame-swallower replied. "His speech sure isn't from the upper class," I noted immediately.

"You so lovely, Kimi. I no lie to girl so sweet. I no Prince." Both girls looked shocked.

"You're not a Prince?" Kimi Kai`ika sounded horrified.

"You forgive Teri'i?" The firedancer begged. He looked deeply into Kimi's eyes. "Teri'i's heart break if no forgive."

The kid had a good line. His looks were great, too. Six foot four, and muscles like Hercules. The stock-broker's wives would go bananas over him, I knew. I wondered if he could sing.

"Why did you say you were a Prince, then, if you're not?"

"Need job. Tourists like Polynesian Revues. In Kauai, where Teri'i learn fire-dance, all good fire-dancers Princes from some Polynesian island."

I laughed. The kid had an innate understanding of show business. "Prince Teri'i," we would headline him. "Just recently arrived from Tahiti."

"Well, what are you then, if you're not a Prince?" the other hula maiden asked, sounding exasperated. She was a beauty, too, but in a different way than Kimi Kai`ika. She looked part Hawaiian but Caucasian features suggested another background as well. "Maybe Portuguese," I surmised.

"Felice Santos," another good name for show business," I decided. "Maybe I can star her in my Latin-American numbers. "Direct from Rio," I could see her billed as "the Latin-American bombshell, Felicia Santos." I didn't think she would mind my changing her first name slightly.

"Teri'i simple vanilla farmer, Felice, from Tahiti," my fire dancer confessed. "But force leave Tahiti. Too many brudders. Not enuff land go round. Come Kauai. Visitors say make big bucks America. Come Makee Plantation, Kauai. But Teri'i no like job. All day, dawn to dark, load sugarcane on train, paid dollar an hour. Buy food Plantation store. Owe mo end of month dan make."

"Are you from Tahiti too, Ito?"

Teri'i laughed.

"No Japanese people in Tahiti, Felice. Some Chinese come work cotton plantation but Ito-san from Honolulu." I noticed Felice eyeing Ito up and down.

"You from Honolulu, Felice-san?" the Japanese kid beamed appreciatively at my Latin-American future star.

"Why, yes, Ito. How did you know?"

"Most beautiful girls in the world in Honolulu, Felice. Better looking than any geisha girl I've seen in Tokyo, for sure." I could tell he had a lot of practice with young women, too. Felice blushed with pleasure.

"How did you learn fire-dancing, Teri'i?" Kimi demanded.

"Already know Tamure, Kimi, fast Tahitian dance. Go Lihue, get second job to midnight. Dance Tamure, Polynesian Revue. Study fire dancers and flame swallower. Go back Plantation, practice outside bunkhouse while others sleep. Get good. See ad in paper."

"You mean you've never had a job as a fire dancer before? Why, your arms are all covered with burn marks," Kimi's eyes welled with tears. Teri'i lapped up the sympathy. He patted her hand.

"No worry, Kimi. Good now, not so many burns."

"Kimi, forget Teri'i's troubles," Felice interrupted. "It's after nine. The audition's are going to start any minute. What are we going to do? You still haven't thought of anything we can dance to."

"Do Tamure, Felice," Ito directed. "Teri'i-san, show Kimi, Felice how to do Tamure."

Teri'i stood up.

"Good idea, Ito-san." He stood up, towering over the girls.

"See, like dis. Teri'i show Kimi, Felice." The fire dancer pulled both girls to their feet. He looked extremely senuous as he bent his knees and rolled his hips to the same rhythm he danced to. The girls looked horrified.

"My father would kill me if I did that in public," Felice protested.

"Tourists like," Teri'i argued. "Study Polynesian revues, Kauai. See hula girls dance Tahitian style. Coconut shells on breasts twirl. Tight-fitting grass skirts. See-trough. Tourists love."

"Teri'i's right, girls," the ukelele player added. "I guarantee you'll be hired if you do the Tahitian Tamure like Teri'i-san says."

I chuckled. The kids had an innate sense of what customers wanted. I popped up from behind the palm tree.

"Mr. Emory," the girls looked mortified.

"Teri'i and Ito are right, girls," I assured them.

"Do that Tahitian Tamure again, Teri'i," I requested. He obliged and several other hula hopefuls gathered around.

"Do that again, Teri'i." He repeated his instruction.

"Try that style, ladies," I ordered. Kimi and Felice watched Teri'i closely and imitated him to a "T." It was just what I wanted.

"Now the rest of you try it," I said to the other hula hopefuls.

"We'll just have to do it Felice," Kimi looked desperate. She dragged her friend over and imitated Teri'i's style again. She looked great. Felice and the others imitated her.

"That's wonderful girls," I encouraged.

Before long we had the whole line of entertainers doing the Tahitian Tamure, with my flame-swallower leading the line. Guests from the hotel were lining up just to watch.

"What do you think of that style of dancing?" I asked a portly, banker-type, his cocktail in hand.

"Why, it's wonderful," he said. "Nothing like a little foreign culture to brighten up your day."

I waved the entertainers into the ballroom. Teri'i's drummers from the night before had arrived.

"Try the Tamure with the drummers," I ordered.

The drummers livened up the ballroom. My burgeoning chorus line followed Teri'is lead and strained to keep up the pace as the drumming accelerated. Kimi and Felice were keeping right up.

"You're all hired," I announced.

"Leave your names with the Hotel desk. I'll be setting up rehearsals starting next week," I promised.

"Now if only I could come up with some old tunes from the Hawaiian past," I thought. "Maybe then I could get on with this revue."

Chapter 7.

Mission International.

"Mrs. Atherton Scully?" the secretary asked, appraising me. I nodded.

"Mr. Baker will see you now, Mrs. Scully."

The secretary led the way to Uncle Norman's opulent office. As she opened the door I could see father's old friend hanging up his phone.

"What an impressive office, Uncle Norman," I told him. "Why, you must be so proud of that polished Koa desk and those Gauguin originals on the walls."

The distinguished businessman stood up and reached for my hand. He gave it a caress with his lips that was anything but fatherly. I glanced more closely at him. The Chief Executive Officer of every Board of Directors of any importance in Hawaii certainly didn't look his age.

"Why, he remains as good-looking as I've always known him," I thought. "With his height, powerful frame and only slightly greying hair."

"He looks younger than Atherton," I thought with shock. "And yet he was born in the same year as my father. How could that be?"

Uncle Norman smiled a thoroughly charming smile. My heart warmed towards him. I found myself repressing my feelings as my body responded to Uncle Norman's considerable sex appeal. I became very aware that his wife had passed away several months ago.

"I wonder if he's found someone else?" I found myself thinking. I had always been impressed with Norman Baker's powerful business mind. I had secretly envied Dorothy Baker, his late wife, for years.

"And to think that I'm stuck with Atherton and an occasional fling with Michael Bridgewater when Norman Baker might be available," I found myself thinking. Shock flooded my mind at my unexpected musing.

"It's because Atherton is so busy," I told myself but the traitorous thoughts kept coming.

"Why, it's close to a month now since Atherton felt like making love. No wonder my body is reacting to an outstandingly attractive member of the opposite sex. I never really knew the real Atherton until Father's death."

"That's when Atherton turned into a wimp," I could swear my body was talking to me. "When your father died and he was fired. Why don't you try a real man for a change?" Such thoughts. I couldn't believe it. I forced myself to quell my rising libido. Uncle Norman was having a totally unexpected impact on me.

"Welcome, Jessica," Uncle Norman boomed. His voice was just as powerful as his frame.

"Please don't address me as Uncle. After all we're not really related. The 'uncle' title was just bestowed on me by your father. Besides, I confess it makes me feel my age."

"You don't look anywhere near your age, Norman," I reassured him." He beamed.

"How nice of you to come down in person to tell me your impressions of how our new Tropical Palace Hotel is doing, Jessica. It's of the utmost importance to me that the Tropical Palace facilities make a first class impression on our invited guests on the Malolo. Tell me My Dear, how is that husband of yours doing with his deadlines?"

I pulled my mind back to business and tried to ignore the strong feelings of attraction I was experiencing in response to Norman's powerful body.

"Atherton is managing as well as can be expected, Norman," I managed. "He's pulled Housekeeping,Grounds, Dining and Beach Facilities into order, my spies at the Hotel tell me. Even my father wouldn't be able to find fault with those facilities now. But I'm not as confident Atherton can handle the music problem by the time the Malolo gets here."

"What seems to be the trouble now, Jessica? I thought we had that music problem under control. I understood the new Music Director I suggested arrived the other day."

"Thank Heavens Norman can't read my mind," I thought as I found myself removing my suit jacket to reveal my considerable natural attributes.

"It's so hot, today, Norman," I complained.

"Let me get you something cool to drink, My Dear." Norman strolled over to his well stocked office bar and poured some liquid over the ice he'd placed in a glass. He made himself one too and brought the drinks over to his desk.

I had a sip and tried to concentrate on what Norman was saying. I was hoping the unexpected impact he was having would go away.

"That's part of the problem," I tried to bring my mind back on business. "Winston Emory seems to know his music all right but from what I could see at last night's auditions, he's floundering in the morass of musical variety that Hawaii has spawned."

"It's vital we change the music in the Ballroom. Patrons have been complaining about it for months."

"Well, it's no wonder, if what I saw last night is representative of what's been playing in the Tropical Palace Ballroom."

A short laugh came out of my mouth as I remembered the awful talent I'd witnessed at the auditions.

"Can you imagine? I had to sit through a rendition of "Yacky Hula Hickey Dula."

"Really?" Norman chuckled. "Not 'Yacky Hula Hickey Dula.' Why that Al Jolson tune went out of date years ago."

"Yes, and it was followed by 'Oh, how she could wicky, wacky, woo.'"

"Now I can uke and uke and uke, and you can uke a ukulele too, and I can wick and you can wack, and we can wicki wicki wacki woo," Norman sang.

Both of us dissolved into gales of laughter. The song selection was so ludicrous.

"How contagious your laughter is, My Dear. You really must come to see me more often. I don't think I've laughed like that since the start of Dorothy's illness."

Norman moved closer. The subtle scent of his expensive aftershave made Norman seem even more appealing.

"An older man," I thought. I forced myself to pull my mind back from it's rather pleasant musing.

"I was so embarrassed for Hawaii's music community, I could have died."

"Heavens, My Dear, those songs were hits in Waikiki for years but I can't imagine any Hotel entertainers playing them today."

My heart picked up it's beat as Norman continued to chat with me. It was like we had been good friends for years. He moved his gaze and I felt his look of appreciation as his eyes travelled discreetly all over my body.

"He's finding me attractive, too," I noted.

"Now tell me Jessica," Norman ordered. "Michael Bridgewater tells me you've inherited a lot of your father's business acumen. How can we help that Music Director?"

I pulled my mind back to the problem at hand. Somehow it seemed very important to me that I not sound like an idiot to Norman.

"Atherton told me before I came that Winston Emory asked him to find someone who's familiar with authentic, Hawaiian music from the old days. It seems that Emory's greatest musical successes are medleys anchored firmly in some way by historical themes. I tried some of my friends but they specialise in European, operetta-type music like the Royal Hawaiian Band plays."

"We don't need any more of that music, My Dear. As nice as it is, Hololulu is saturated with it. No, we need something new and original." Norman seemed to go deeply into thought.

"If Winston Emory wants a theme, I think I can supply him with one."

My heart raced slightly again. The Chief Executive Officer sounded so confident and powerful. I was always attracted to decisive men. It was one of Atherton's lackings that drove me mad.

"Jessica," Norman said warmly. "You know how your father and I were pleased with our importation of four hundred thousand workers for the Plantations. That was because we always felt that God had a special destiny in mind when He allowed American Puritans to gather much of the good farm land in Hawaii away from those non-productive Kanakas."

Norman told me that my father and him were convinced that God had a special purpose in mind for Hawaii when it became possible to bring such large amounts of Asians into the Islands. Norman said that both father and he were convinced that with the rapid assimilation of Asiatic peoples that had been managed on the Plantations, Hawaii had a role to act as a bridge between the East and the West. Norman claimed that Hawaii was meant to act as a catalyst to bring the Eastern Nations like China and Japan more in line with Western thinking and Capitalist styles of doing business."

"I can remember you and my father having long conversations about that."

"And now our new Tourist Industry is doing well, too, despite the depression on the mainland. I'm positive Hawaii is meant to act as a leader in the International scene. As a model of peaceful cooperation between peoples of the East and peoples of the West. And beyond that as a example of how American Capitalism should be the goal for this large planet of ours."

I marvelled at the scope of Norman's mind. He was everything my husband was not.

"Perhaps your husband could suggest that as a theme to our new Music Director. Something like, 'Hawaii's Hidden Destiny.' Why, there's already been conferences held here on Hawaii's role in international politics."

"Having met the young man I don't think Winston Emory's going to accept direct suggestions. He's more the type that likes to think he's discovered a theme himself, from old music or traditions, I believe."

"You've always been an excellent judge of character."

"Why, thank you. No one's ever said such a thing to me before. I've always left such matters to Atherton in the past but since Father died I've felt it necessary to take a more direct role in business affairs. After all, Father did leave everything in my name."

Norman gave a slight chuckle.

"Very wise of him, My Dear. Perhaps we could arrange for that Music Director of ours to meet some Hawaiian musicians, just as he's requested. Some of our own choosing, of course."

"Norman, what are you suggesting?"

My father's old friend picked up the phone. I stared at Norman admiring his problem solving ability.

"Miss Swanson," he spoke to his secretary.

"Connect me to Dr. Rosalie Switzer at the Museum. I've got a task for her."

"Don't worry about the music problem any longer Jessica. This is a chance to protect our investment in the Hotel hui and further your father's and my interest in a prestigious role for Hawaii in International affairs."

"Rosalie, My Dear, Norman Baker here."

I started as I found myself feeling unreasonably jealous at Norman calling another woman "My Dear." I listened to their conversation with great interest.

"Thank you for gracing my dinner party the other night. You

were the talk of my friends for days. They all wanted to know who the mysterious academic was."

"I'm afraid I must throw myself on your mercy for a favor. I'll get right to the point, I know how busy you are. In all the Hawaiian kupunas you've interviewed do you recall someone familiar with authentic Hawaiian songs dating back into the late 1800's and early 1900's? Someone who might be willing to share their knowledge with the new Music Director of the Tropical Palace Hotel?"

"You do, how wonderful. An old lady out in the Panini Valley, you say, Auntie Edith Hoaloha. I know this sounds like an odd question but do you happen to know how she feels about tourism?"

"Oh, she's an exception to most of the old Kanakas, is she? Likes to see the old music passed on and played by local musicians for the tourists, you say? That's odd. Most of those Kanakas guard their music like jealous sheep dogs."

"Thinks it's a way to keep the old heritage alive, eh? Sounds like the person we need to send our new Music Director out to see. Can you look up her exact location and relay it to my secretary. I can assure you I'll be forever grateful to you."

After a little more small talk Norman hung up the phone.

"Well, My Dear, our new Music Director is going to have a special interview with an ancient Hawaiian musician and perhaps some more people who think like her as well. Dr. Switzer says that Auntie Edith Hoaloha is quite unique. She doesn't keep her music underground at all like so many of the older Kanaka families do. Thinks she has a special mission to pass on the old heritage to preserve it. We'll give her a hand." Norman winked at me.

"Have Atherton suggest a special theme for a new music medley, too. Something like the old Hawaiian gods proclaiming that our Islands have a special mission to entertain and welcome visitors from all over the world."

"That sounds like a line from the Hawaii Tourist Bureau."

"Of course, Jessica. What other message would we want to give our wealthy stockbrokers on the Malolo."

"Just give me the rest of the day. Rosalie's sending a runner up to the Panini settlement to let Auntie Edith know another recorder is coming to put her music into written form. I'll get a message through to Atherton about when and where to send a driver and the young man."

I fell into silence admiring the way Norman had so quickly solved the music crisis.

"By the way, My Dear," my heart pounded as Norman moved close again. "On a more personal note, you look devastating in that lovely, cream-colored blouse that sets off your physical attributes so well. Would you possibly do me the honor of being my hostess at a private dinner for one of my Board of Directors one week from today. It would give me so much pleasure."

"Why Norman, what an honour." I prayed my face had not gone as red as it felt. I felt my self-esteem soar at Norman's request. What a coup! An invitation to Norman's dinner table was a command performance for Hawaii's elite. Any of my high-society friends would give their right arm to act as Norman's offical hostess. Why, Norman Baker was held in even greater esteem than Michael Bridgewater.

"Of course, only if Atherton will spare you for the occasion? Michael Bridgewater tells me your husband likes to keep you under wraps, all to himself."

Norman gave me a searching look. Irritation at the way Atherton had been hiding out from society since his firing flowed through my veins.

"I can speak for myself, Norman," I protested. "Besides I'm sure Atherton wouldn't mind. He spends most of his evenings now trying to get the hotel up to the highest standards."

"How admirable of him. I'll send my car for you then, Tuesday at 6:00 p.m., precisely. Perhaps you could contact my housekeeper, Mrs. Blennings and take control of the dinner menu."

We stood up and Norman came close and helped me on with my suit jacket. He gave me a gentle kiss on my cheek. Our bodies touched lightly and I felt myself quivering with expectation. It had been so long since I had wanted a man to pull me against him.

"Until next Tuesday, then, Jessica," Norman whispered quietly as his secretary appeared in the doorway. "Your presence will give me such pleasure."

I went out to my waiting car feeling strangely invigorated.

"Could such a man be interested in me?" I found myself musing on the way home. "Why, Norman Baker is everything Atherton is not."

Chapter 8.

Passing On The Old Music.

I sighed as I realised I was going to have to leave the calming influence of the surf and sand to return to my now odious task as Music Director. I procrastinated and inhaled deeply, savoring the odour of Plumeria flying vigorously in the brisk trade winds that day. Finally I managed to resign myself to another eight or ten hours of work. I was not making much headway in Paradise.

"If only there was a way to figure out which stocks on the market were going to increase and which were not?" I mused. "Then I wouldn't have to work for a living. I could just laze all day in Paradise." A full week had passed and I still had not come up with enough inspiration to even work on an outline for the new revue. Without it, I realised that my days in Paradise were numbered.

"Thank God for Ito and Teri'i, though," I sighed. They are shaping up the hula dancers quite nicely. The whole troupe could now do a spirited Tahitian Tamure in perfect rhythm.

"Maybe that will be enough to keep Atherton Scully from sending me back to New York," I thought.

"Ito and Teri'i are so typical of entertainers," I tried to think of something cheerful. They are pursuing Kimi Kai`ika and Felice Santos as if their lives depended on it. But the girls are so resistant. My mind went back to the scene at the rehearsal last night.

"Kimi go visit Kauai wit Teri'i?" he had asked so hopefully.
"Teri'i want show Kimi 'Spouting Horn.'"
"Sorry, Teri'i," she had poured cold water onto his plans. "Felice and I have something more important to do."
"What more important than Teri'i and Ito-san?" my Tahitian Prince demanded. I could tell he was not used to rejection from the opposite sex.
"Oh, it's nothing personal. I'd love to see the sights of Kauai with you but Felice and I have to report to the University during the day. The Territorial Normal School has us taking part in it's bonding program."
"University? Wat bonding program?" Teri'i sounded extremely disappointed.
"It's pretty sad," Kimi tried to explain. "Dr. Curtis, the Director of the teaching program is trying to get all of the students to bond, so they can be helpful to each other when they become actual teachers. But none of the other teachers are willing to bond with Felice and I. We're the only non-Haole and non-Japanese students. I guess Felice and I will have to bond with each other."
"Kimi, Felice become teachers!" Teri'i voice was full of horror. "No way. Kimi, Felice be entertainers like Ito-san and Teri'i. No be teachers!"
"Teri'i-san, teaching is an honorable profession," Ito tried to rescue his partner before he hopelessly offended Kimi.
"No way," Teri'i was not catching the cues Ito was trying to throw. "Teachers be old maids. Kimi, Felice no meant be old maids."
"Teri'i, what do you have against teachers?" I could tell by her voice that Kimi was becoming quite irritated. "After all someone taught you to read and write, I'm sure."
"Vitori not learn read, write. Papeete School teach only in French. Teri'i only speak Tahitian. Papeete School teach only bout French history. Run away. Papeete school no let Students speak Tahitian. Same here Hawaii? Kimi be too sweet, no punish students speak Hawaiian."

"It's different here, Teri'i," Kimi protested.

"No it's not," Felice jumped into the conversation. "Hawaiian kids can't speak Hawaiian in school here, either. And plantation kids aren't allowed to speak pidgin English in school like they do with all their friends. Dr. Curtis said so, himself, yesterday."

"You're right, Felice," Ito joined in. "I got my hands struck many times for speaking Japanese to my friends in school. Then I got punished for speaking English at the Japanese school my father insisted I go to in the afternoons. Maybe you will come with Teri'i-san and me to Kauai and see Waimea Canyon, Hanalei Bay and the Wailua Falls. Perhaps we could go on a weekend?"

"I would love to, Ito. Let's go the first time the Tropical Palace gives us a weekend off."

"Felice, Kimi protested. "You know how buried under we are with assignments. We haven't got time to go off on some sightseeing trip to Kauai."

"Speak for yourself, Kimi." I could Felice was responding to Ito's considerable charm.

"Teri'i, Ito-san take Felice, Kauai," Teri'i promised. "First time hotel geev days off." I could tell he was trying to make Kimi jealous.

My mind drifted away from young love back to my predicament as Music Director of the Tropical Palace Hotel.

"Even with the Tahitian Tamure, what did I have for opening night?" I sighed. I realised that the hula troupe, Kimi Kai`ika and Felice Santos would thrill the stock-brokers. I gambled that Alan Carstairs, the Irish tenor and Tahitian Prince Teri'i would make all the stock-brokers wives' hearts throb, but I knew I was still lacking a theme for the new revue. I could tell it would have to have something to do with old Hawaii but I marvelled that I was supposed to function without knowing what the old music was like.

"Yacky Hula Hickey Dula," I recalled the tune that had Jessica Scully choking on her cocktail. "Perhaps it does have possibilities," I thought. "At least the sheet music for it is available. Maybe with a Tahitian rhythm?"

"Christ, I've reached the bottom of the barrel," I realised.

"Mr. Scully wants you to report to his office," the Bartender informed me. "After you've eaten this crab salad." He placed the lunch of the day in front of me.

"The boss says you'll need some nourishment where you're going."

"My God." I panicked. "A return trip to New York, I bet." I could mentally hear the ship in Honolulu harbor signalling it's boarding call. I gulped down the meal and bolted to Scully's office.

"Get that worried expression off your face, Emory."

My boss gave me an appraising look as I entered his den.

"My wife has come up with a solution to your sheet music problems. Go home and gather some clothes. Enough for a week or so. You're going to visit Auntie Edith Hoaloha out in Panini Valley."

"How did you manage that Mr. Scully?" I asked, excitement filling my mind. "I'll be forever grateful to your wife."

"Just make sure you take enough empty sheet music with you Emory. Jessica found this lady somehow. Now you go out there and come back with ideas for a new review. You said you wanted history and now you're going to get it."

"What about my rehearsals, Mr. Scully? I've got choreography set for every day this week."

"That young Tahitian Prince can take over in your absence, Emory. Regulars at the bar are wild about his Tahitian Tamure. I like his style and I know you're training your dance girls to do the Tamure. And I like that comic hula your Japanese ukelele player is teaching them to do."

I sighed a deep breath of relief. My confidence flowed back.

"One Hawaiian revue coming up Mr. Scully."

"One word of warning, Emory. Don't let that Kanaka Auntie know you're going to make changes to the dances and music she's showing you. She thinks you're recording the old music for posterity, as part of the Museum project. Understand?"

"I get it, Mr. Scully. I'll record the old music all right. But then I'll make my own adaptations, like a western rhythm that can be danced to, and a theme that mainstream Americans can relate to, like Boy meets Girl, or something like that."

"Excellent, Emory. Norman Baker asked me to pass on a couple of themes to you, too. One is Hawaii as Paradise, destined to lure peoples from all over the world. His second theme is far too ambitions, though, if you ask me. An International role for Hawaii, to act as a bridge between the East and the West. Anyway the car's out front. Good luck."

I went back to my suite and loaded a suitcase full of clothes, blank sheet music and several forty ouncers of the strongest rum I could locate. I carried the bulging suitcase out of the front entrance of the Hotel. A taxi with a uniformed driver was at my beck and call. He placed my suitcase in the trunk.

"Aunt Edith Hoaloha's place in Panini Valley," I told the driver. He was a Filipino looking fellow with highly polished black shoes.

"Sure Brah," he responded. "Carlos take you Panini Valley." He headed leisurely out onto Kalakaua Avenue.

"You know someone Panini Valley?" he asked, curiousity getting the better of him. "Dat Hawaiian squatters' land. You no type go dere."

My heart skipped a couple of beats. Hawaiian squatters' land. What had I got myself into.

"An invitation I couldn't refuse," I tried to hide my growing fears from the driver. "Have you been there before, Carlos?"

"Go Panini Valley all time, Brah. Carlos take Kanakas back and forth Panini Valley, like pingpong balls. Panini Brahs not know if dey wan be country folk or city folk."

"What do you mean?"

"Oh, old Kanakas stay Panini. But young Brahs and wahines

no like live primitive ways in old shanty-town. They tink mo to life dan fish and poi."

"Shanty-town?" I said in consternation. Primitive-like?" I could see Carlos grin in the front mirror.

"No tink dos Brahs your type," he laughed.

"There is modern plumbing there, isn't there?"

"No way, Brah. No toilet, sink, lights, phone, no road, just trail go up mountain and shacks."

"My God," I exclaimed in horror. "A week without electricity or plumbing. And I can't even phone for someone to get me out of there?"

"No worry Brah. Carlos look out fo you. Wen take Brahs, wahines, children, back and forth."

"Take flag." He handed me a flag of some country. I supposed it was from the Philipines. "You want ride, hang from roof. I watch. Be OK."

"How come there's so much back and forth movement?" I asked.

"Old Kanakas stay Panini. But young brahs, wahines come down City. Get jobs pineapple cannery, construction, hotels. Money flow til big surf or luau time. Mo important den job. Quit, party, come back relatives. Always room in pili grass shacks. I move children, dogs, chickens, pigs, back Panini."

"Don't employers get tired of workers coming and going? Where do they stay in the city?"

"Squat by sea, Brah. Fish, gather limu. Rent slum tenements wen can afford. Come, go, party bigtime on beach. Life one big luau until quit."

"How do they survive?" I queried, appalled at such an unstable lifestyle. Don't the children go to school?"

"No point, Brah. Students never pass. Hard learn reading, writing. No speak English. Just feel bad wen fail all time. Most never even pass grade school. Speak pidgin like Carlos. Only Haoles, educated Chinese, Japanese get jobs. Why I drive taxi, Brah. Save many years Plantation. Father help."

I nodded, not understanding why anyone would live in primitive conditions in this day and age.

"You have walk up trail to top Valley, Brah. Auntie Edith old lady. First squatter in Panini. Choose ridge. Say can speak to gods better. Car no go up dere."

I groaned as I thought of the weight of my suitcase. No plumbing. I was sorely tempted to tell the driver to turn around and go back to the Hotel. But then I thought of Jessica Scully, the state of my bank account, and the hopelessness of employment for bandless music directors in the mainland depression.

"I suppose this is my last chance to find the old tunes that will allow me to put the revue together," I thought. I resigned myself to a week in Hell.

I didn't have long for it to start. The good road suddenly disappeared and I found myself at the start of a meandering trail that only a sure-footed mule could negotiate.

"See thatched house in distance, Brah?" I stared forlornly into the lush tropical valley.

"Up," the driver pointed towards a cluster of old grass and plywood shacks.

"Up further, Brah." I moved my head slowly up where he was pointing.

"My God," I gasped. A huge grass shack could be seen precariously clinging to a ridge.

"House, Auntie Edith Hoaloha," Carlos laughed.

"Promise you'll check for your flag hanging everytime you come out?" I begged. "And come back to pick me up one week from today?"

"Sure Brah. If you still be in one piece. Some big Kanakas no aloha for Haoles from mainland," he warned. Dey say Haoles steal dere land."

"How preposterous," I remarked.

"Not so sure, Brah. 1850 American missionaries convince Kanaka king put all land fo sale Hawaii. Say geev some to Kanakas but dey have pay fo land transfer one third value.

Kanakas no have money. Missionaries, udder foreigners buy most land from king."

Carlos drove off and my own worries took me away from the land problems of Hawaiians.

"What happened to paradise luring people from all over the world?" I thought of Norman Baker's suggestion for a theme as Carlos disappeared. I dragged my heavy suitcase up the trail to the first of the plywood shacks. Within seconds I became surounded by a mob of Hawaiian kids, a barking, howling, pack of dogs and more wild chickens than I had ever seen in my life. A few pigs joined the happy scene.

I cursed out loud at Jessica Scully. "This was her idea, I know it," I thought. Horror stories of missing tourists in foreign countries flooded my mind. "Will my parents even know what happened to me?" I panicked.

"Auntie Edith Hoaloha?" I yelled in desperation.

"You friend Auntie, Brah?" One of the largest of the boys demanded.

"Definitely," I replied.

"Why you no say so?" His glare broke into a smile and the others followed his example.

"Up top, Brah. See house top Valley?" I followed his hand signal. The house looked even farther than it had from the road.

Somehow I knew my scrawny body was not going to be up to dragging my suitcase up that trail. I hadn't done anything more strenuous in years than wave a baton to conduct an orchestra.

Just then a horse-drawn cart pulled in from the main road. It was driven by an ancient-looking Chinese fellow with a pigtail at the back of his head. He had a load of fresh vegetables taking up the space at the back of his cart. I pulled out a bill from my pocket.

"Any chance of getting a ride to the top?" I requested, waving the bill in front of his face.

"Ah Chun take you," the old fellow reached for the bill eagerly.

He pointed to the back of the cart. My suitcase and I barely found room among the turnips, lettuce and potatoes.

"Tell wahines Ah Chun bring veggies later," he told the urchins. We jolted up the long trail.

"Horse not used to extra weight," the old fellow complained. I handed him another bill. He said something to the old horse in Chinese and I swear the old horse strained to pick up his pace slightly.

"Probably threatened to make it a gelding," I thought.

I sighed and stared at the assortment of shanties along the trail. Some of them were constructed out of old boards but many of them were grass shacks. I'd never seen such a collection of shanties, not even in the slums of New York.

Grass huts became more frequent the further we went up the steep trail. The grass and plywood shacks came in all shapes and sizes. The huts were teeming with bare-footed children dressed in the least possible amount of clothing. Assorted chickens, pigs, dogs and cats raised quite a ruckus as the old cart rolled slowly up the mountain.

I noticed taro planted wherever water could be brought through viaducts. Mango, papaya, and orange trees grew in profusion. Tropical flowers were everywhere. The old horse finally reached the end of the trail.

"Ah Chun," a weathered old lady came out of a grass shack.

"I knew it," I sighed to myself. "More Hula Kahiko." I groaned in dispair.

"Aloha Auntie," Ah Chun chuckled. "You have visitor."

"Aloha Winslun," the old lady cackled. I started. "How the Hell does she know my name?" I wondered.

"Welcome Panini Valley. You student?" the old lady cackled. "Dr. Switzer say student come. Study music, my ohana? But how come look older dan student?"

"Winston Emory, Mrs. Hoaloa," I smiled my most charming smile. "I was accepted by the University as a mature student," I lied.

"No Mrs. Hoaloha, Winslun," she laughed. "Auntie Edith." She smiled a nearly toothless grin.

"Doctor say you stay week. I play ukelele, chant old songs of ohana." I suddenly thought of my stomach.

"A week without the Hotel Dining room? How will I survive?" The old lady must have read my mind.

"No worry, Winslun! Auntie feed. Good fish, poi." I resigned myself to a week of starvation.

"Not poi," I thought. I'd had a taste of it at the Hotel. It resembled wallpaper paste and tasted just like it to me. I groaned.

The old lady led me inside her hut. I prepared myself for the worst. I expected fleas, lice and rats inside all that grass. I started with surprise.

The hut was immaculate. An ornate, pandanus mat covered the floor over a bed of perfectly matched tiny pebbles. Cooking utensils were neatly hanging on the walls as were several ukeleles, guitars and drums. I groaned as gourds of different sizes and shapes were displayed as well.

"Not a week of the Hula Kahiko," I prayed.

"You sleep heah." The old lady pointed to one half of the hut. I put my suitcase down wearily against the wall.

"No worry, Winslun. Hawaiian people happy people. You see." And so began my education in Hawaiian music.

The old lady lost no time. She motioned me to come out of her house and went over and banged a metal triangle with a long stick. The sound reverberated down the valley like a gong.

"We start, Winslun. I summon dancers. I show you all types chant and hula." I winced as she picked up a gourd like the one from the other night as well as several other instruments I didn't recognise.

"Dis ipu, Winslun. Used for hula." She handed me another instrument. It was a wooden drum covered in shark-skin. "Dis temple drum Winslun. Use fo sacred chant. Only tree, four chants use temple drum."

Auntie led me up a trail going even higher up the ridge. I

staggered under the weight of the temple drum and other assorted instruments in a huge duffle bag. Before long we came to some kind of stone platform.

"This old heiau (temple), Winslun. Auntie speak Hawaiian gods. You show respect."

I glanced at the old temple. All that remained was a stone platform. I looked at some of the stones holding the platform. They were huge.

"I wonder how they got those stones away up here," I wondered.

I looked down and could see Hawaiians dressed in what must have been the costumes of old working their way up the trail towards us.

Auntie waited until the dancers caught up to us and chose one of the younger ladies from the group.

"Dis Noelani," she said. "She be translator." Auntie motioned us to the side of the stone platform.

Auntie moved to the other side of the stone platform and motioned the dancers onto the stage. There were about twelve dancers, ten females and two males. Auntie started to chant, sounding much like the old crone from the auditions the other day.

"This prayer," my interpreter told me. "Auntie asking Hawaiian gods for protection from evil. Gods names Hi`iaka, Pele, Laka, Kanaloa."

"How do you spell those?" I wrote the names of the gods down. I listened intently. Auntie's voice quality was unlike anything I had ever heard in western music. Her voice quavered eerily. Sometimes it was a faint whisper and then her voice would become very powerful unexpectedly.

"Kapu (sacredness) and mana (power) of chant is in its words," my young interpreter told me. She looked very serious.

"Auntie calling on Laka, goddess of the hula for protection. You must pay attention to the kaona, the hidden meaning of the words."

"Oh, great," I thought. "I can't understand a word the old lady is saying and I'm supposed to be aware of hidden meanings. Must be the opposite of Hollywood here. No one has to worry about the meaning of songs there."

Auntie's voice stopped suddenly. She appeared to go into a trance of some kind. She was silent for a few minutes then leaped to her feet with a whirl of incantations of some kind. The other dancers imitated her chanting and movements.

"Auntie doing more prayer," my interpreter said. "She pray for Divine inspiration."

The dancers continued for some time. It looked like the whole works of them were in some kind of trance. I found the performance quite eery.

Finally Auntie left the platform and sat down beside the temple drum I'd carried up the mountain.

"That temple drum," my interpreter told me. "Auntie do praise to gods again."

The rhythm of the chant had changed completely. But it was still not similar to western music. The dancers were impressive, swaying in exact thythm with the drums. I noticed their hand and foot movements were quite intricate.

At the end of that particular chant Auntie set aside the drum and picked up what appeared to be some small lava rocks.

"This hula `ila`ila," my helper explained. "Small lava rocks."

I was fascinated by the rhythm Auntie produced with the rocks. "Something like castinets," I thought. "If I can only change the rhythm and set it to music with harmony that is pleasant to western ears."

Auntie's rhythm changed again as she went back to her large gourd.

"This final dance, a prayer of thanks," my interpreter said. I sighed a sigh of relief. The sacred chant had been fascinating but I could see I'd never be able to present it to western ears.

I thanked the dancers and Auntie. The dancers disappeared down the trail again. Auntie brought me back to her house.

"Auntie want you see all types of sacred hula, Winslun. You record for Dr. Switzer?"

"Yes, Auntie," I lied.

"How did the sacred chanting get preserved without written form all these years?" I asked.

"Each Island, Winslun, family chosen dance for high chiefs. Pass chants on to relatives." Auntie gave me a lecture on the history of the hula. She told me that missionaries had come to Hawaii in 1820 and soon convinced the high chiefs they converted to ban the hula. Auntie told me that the hula didn't completely disappear, it went underground. She told me that it was never done for westerners and that King Kamehameha V in the 1860's and King Kalakaua in the 1880's defied the missionaries and sponsored hula. The kings allowed public hula but when Hawaii became a U. S. Territory,in 1902, hula and chant were made illegal, like the speaking of the Hawaiian language. Auntie said that the Americans were determined to turn all Hawaiians into Haoles. At that time hula went underground again and was performed only for Hawaiians.

I sat down on my side of the pandanus mat in Auntie's house. I opened my suitcase, pulled out the two glasses I'd had the foresight to include and poured us each a generous portion of the high alcohol content rum.

"Later, Winslun, I still speak Hawaiian Gods. Must honor. No drink yet. Make Pele angry. House go down trail in landslide."

I hastily poured the liquor back into the bottle.

The old lady banged on her ipu in a rhythm distressing to my ears and started chanting in the old style. I couldn't understand a word she was saying but I didn't want to tempt Pele or whoever it was that could cause a landslide. I listened stoically.

After minutes that seemed like hours to my ears, Auntie stopped.

"You no write, Winslun?" she asked. "Udder students, Doctor send, dey record."

"I can't understand the language, Auntie," I complained.

"Other students write Hawaiian," the old lady said suspiciously.

"Translate for me please, Auntie," I begged.

Another incredibly long hour went by. The old lady translated but the words didn't seem to be anything that could be adapted into ballroom dance music soothing to western ears. However, I dutifully wrote down everything she said. I didn't want to blow my cover. Atherton Scully had said to look like I was recording the old music verbatim.

"God, these old pieces are monotonous," I thought. "Who wants to hear about lava flows and Gods moving from island to island." I was growing more and more desperate.

"Auntie, aren't there any old songs dating after the missionaries came," I asked.

"Dere are, Winslun, but I say goodbye Hawaiian Gods if you want hear dat music. Not sacred."

"Please Auntie," I begged.

Auntie chanted something in Hawaiian and then put aside her gourd. She picked up a ukelele in its place and started singing in falsetto. I listened closely to the music. It was almost like some combination of a chant and hymns used in a Church service.

"Where did that music come from, Auntie?" I asked.

"From himeni, Winslun. When Missionaries come convert ali`i. Commoners learn hymns in church. Sometimes combine with chanting style. Like dis."

Auntie picked up a ukelele and started strumming. Her beat was march music.

"Dis called 'Sweet Lei Lehua,' Winslun. Henry Berger, Bandmaster Royal Hawaiian Band, compose from humming he hear in street. Lots of tunes like dis lost. Berger not publish. Only arrange for band."

"Now 1900's Winslun. Ragtime. You hear 'Waikiki Mermaid?'

Auntie played something that sounded like a Tin Pan Alley song.

"Sonny Cunha, 1903, Winslun. Also dis one."

Auntie played something about a Honolulu hula girl. Then she broke into "Yacka Hula Hickey Dula." My mind reeled. I felt like I was back with Atherton Scully at the auditions again.

"What the devil am I going to do with this music?" I thought. Then suddenly I thought of Teri'i, the fire dancer and his catchy Tahitian rhythm.

"What about old music from other Polynesian Islands, Auntie?" I dared to interrupt.

The old lady nodded. She exchanged her ukelele for a drum. My eyes lit up. She moved into a number that at least had the semblance of Tahitian rhythm.

"Go slower, Auntie," I commanded. I scribbled furiously. I couldn't keep up with the old lady's pace.

"That music is warlike," I realised. I liked the ferocity of the rhythm. I remembered the hotel musicians playing something like that.

Inspiration finally flowed through my mind.

"The Hawaiian War Chant, I think it's called," I remembered. The Music Director from one of the other hotels has already adapted it. I'll use it in my review. Hawaiians were warriors, I'm sure," I rationalised, thinking of the statue of Kamehameha I, the conquerer of all the Islands displayed across the street from the palace in Honolulu.

"Auntie do you know any more music like that?"

"Sure, Winslun," she laughed. "Why you no ask befo?" More tunes using the Tahitian rhythm and some other rhythm flowed out.

"What kind of music is that, Auntie?"

"Tongan, Samoan, Winslun."

I recorded furiously. By the end of the afternoon I knew I had the solution for the music medley.

"A Polynesian revue," I decided. "Why restrict the music to Hawaii alone. "The tourists will love it and I've already got the dancers and musicians practicing the Tahitian Tamure. Why didn't I think of it before?" I cursed my stupidity.

Finally the old lady stopped her chanting.

"Auntie tired Winslun. We stop now. Do more tomorrow."

"Great Auntie." I realised she had already helped a lot.

The old lady disappeared out the door and came back with a huge wooden bowl of poi and some dried fish. She went back out and brought in an assortment of tropical fruit.

I re-poured the rum.

"To Pele, Winslun," Auntie made a toast.

"To Pele, Auntie." We finished one quarter of the bottle of overproof rum and I ate most of the fruit before we retired for the night.

"You good man, Winslun," Auntie sighed as she moved to her side of the room. You save Ohana music from pau—finish."

I felt guilt flow through me but the rum helped me drift off to sleep without further remorse.

The next morning Auntie started again. She had gone back to Hawaiian chanting. I bore with it for an hour but I knew I wasn't getting anything I could use even with her literal translation into English for me.

"Auntie, stop for a moment," I silenced her.

"Auntie, just tell me what the story is about in your chant. Not word for word, just the main meaning of the story, please. I want to make a summary of it."

"Tell old story, Winslun. About `Ohana leave udder Islands far away cross ocean. After many many day come to new Island. People leave canoe and climb volcano. See sun fill crater—name Haleakala—house of sun. One young kane and wahine explore. Find silversword."

"A silver sword?" I queried.

"No sword, Winslun," Auntie laughed. "Silversword plant. Have long silver spikes. Grow only on Haleakala. Anyway, kahuna dream befo trip. Where silver sword, new home fo Ohana. Kane and wahine know prophecy come true. Can stay. Make home. Others follow young kane. See silver sword. Family gods happy. Dey set up village. Name Island Maui."

I beamed. Suddenly I had a theme western audiences would appreciate. Polynesian romance in a new paradise. My orchestra sounded in my head. I could hear it now. Prince Teri'i and Kimi Kai'ika doing a jazzed up Hawaiian hula up the side of a cleverly designed stage volcano. "Tin Pan Alley, eat your heart out," I laughed.

"Boy meets girl. Joined forever in a new land of Paradise. Hawaii beckons to the world," I thought, thinking of Norman Baker's suggestion for a theme. Perfect. "Come to me, your Paradise awaits." Lyrics were writing themselves in my head.

"Auntie, what other stories do old chants tell?" I asked.

"Why, tell of Kamehameha conquering Oahu, Winslun. Hundreds warriors over cliff, meet death. Kamehameha unite all Islands."

"Chant the story for me, Auntie." She obliged and I feverishly wrote every word down as Auntie stopped to translate. "To heck with the chant," I thought. "I'll just write the melodies and lyrics myself. Then I'll rechoreograph the pieces."

"What are those dancing sticks called, Auntie?" She had pulled some bamboo-type sticks off her wall and was playing a rhythm similar to Prince Teri'i's.

"'Uli, 'uli," she replied.

"I've got to have some of those," I thought. "And those." Auntie had picked up her small lava rocks and duplicated the rhythm with them.

Ila'ila, the interpreter had called them.

"To me they were just like the castinets in my Latin-American numbers," I thought. The stock-brokers will love it.

"Tell me the story of another old chant, Auntie," I requested as she stopped. I couldn't believe my luck had finally changed.

"I hope I've brought along enough sheet music," I thought.

"Chant tell of Pele, Winslun. Goddess of Volcano. From Marquesas. She move Island to Island. Take fire wit her. First Ni'ihau, den Kauai, den Oahu, Maui, Big Island. Follow lover. Battle sister for lover."

"Great Auntie," I encouraged. Romance, migration, Pagan Gods, classic Hollywood themes. I loved it and I knew the wealthy tourists would, too.

"What other Hawaiian Gods?" I asked Auntie.

"Many gods, Winslun. Kane, Kanaloa, Ku, Pele, Hina. All have chants."

I didn't recognise the names, but I was sure the Hotel audience would lap it up if I referred to them as the Rain god, the Wind god, the Sun god. "Just like the Gods of American Indians," I thought. Hollywood already had everyone loving pow wows, war dances, and sun dances.

"Orchestration after orchestration was forming in my head. I knew my problem was solved. "I'll play my adaptations of Polynesian music forever," I vowed. "It's my ticket to paradise."

Every day Auntie added more to my collection of ancient Hawaii music. Every afternoon I rewrote and generated lyrics for the new revue.

"Auntie, what Ke aloha mean?" Every other chant seemed to have Ke aloha in it.

"Aloha love, Winslun. Aloha mean wat deep witin the heart of Hawaiian people."

"How romantic," I thought. "How Hollywoodish."

A romantic, myself, at heart, I had no trouble writing of love under the Hawaiian moon. I wrote of the sound of the surf, the hum of the trade winds, the sounds of guitars and the rush of the wind through Palm trees, as lovers danced beneath the Hawaiian stars. In luxurious Hotel courtyards of course.

"Sunrise, Plumeria, Sunset, Swaying Palms, Brave surfers risking all for love. The unridable wave." I recorded it all. I could see that Hawaii was a treasure trove of romantic themes.

"Come to me," I wrote, watching Auntie's sexual gyrations for some of the old pieces. I didn't have to know exactly what the words were for those. Titles seemed to flow out of the blue. I wrote them down. I'd fill in the melody and lyrics later.

"Thank you Auntie," I hugged my generous benefactor after

a week. Never did I ever want to see fish or poi again but I knew the old lady had given me everything I needed.

"Thank you, Winslun, fo record old chants."

I staggered down the mountain dragging my suitcase full of sheet music after me. I made my way through smiling groups of Hawaiian urchins. I knew Auntie had told them I was saving Hawaiian music. Joy filled me as I spotted Carlos sitting patiently by the last plywood shack.

Carlos picked up my bulging suitcase with a grin.

"Must got wat you came fo, Brah?"

I sank gratefully into the taxi. A sea of smiling faces waved me off as we left.

"Hawaiians have to be one of the happiest people in the world," I remarked.

"Hawaiians never fret," I remembered some more lyrics I had heard in Hawaii. "Hawaiians never worry. They just laze and play all day in Paradise." I knew it was just what the tourists wanted to hear. And at least it suited one of Norman Baker's themes. The new Paradise in the U. S. Territory of Hawaii, a land of Aloha, eagerly awaiting tourists.

"Well?" questioned Atherton Scully as the bellboy staggered off with my suitcase.

"It was just like your wife said, Mr. Scully. I've got enough themes and stories to keep writing for the rest of my life, if necessary."

"What themes, Emory?"

"Why, romance, Hawaiian gods beckoning people from all over the globe to Paradise. Hawaii a place of contentment and enlightenment, a model for Eastern nations to follow, to name a few."

"Excellent Emory. Norman Baker will be pleased. Write that up. I'll take it in for the Sunday newspaper. We'll do some advance publicity for the opening."

Chapter 9.

The Revue.

"Kimi Kai`ika, how did you get so out of shape?" I asked myself as Teri'i, Ito, Felice and I were allowed a fifteen minute break while the rest of the dance troupe practiced the new routines our boss had introduced. I realised I was totally exhausted.

I leaned closer to hear what Teri'i was saying. He was complaining about something. Teri'i was sweating profusely from the workout. I couldn't help noticing that the sweat on his muscles only made him more good looking.

"Boss Emory slavemaster," he complained. "Practice all time since Boss return from week vacation. Worse dan plantation. Work never finish."

Teri'i criticism of our boss irritated me somehow. I tried to point out the good points of our boss. I knew he was a great example of what our Territorial Normal School Principal called a "success by American standards."

"Mr. Emory is an example to all of us, Teri'i," I disagreed with him. I watched the crease on his brow broadening as he frowned. I realised that Teri'i wasn't used to young females correcting him.

"Why Mr. Emory made it to the top of his profession by hard work and individual achievement. He's a real perfectionist. That's what pays off in America. Why, he works harder than everyone else if you ask me. Always coming up with new songs and dance routines. Even the stage crew complain about his constant present on that volcano set they're constructing."

Ito laughed.

"I think Emory-san made it more by figuring out what his American audiences wanted, Kimi, rhythm, looks and romance and making sure they got it."

"Wat perfectionist?" Teri'i sounded irritated. Kimi use long words. No understand."

"Someone who won't stop until what they are doing is perfect," I explained.

"That's Winston Emory all right," Felice sighed.

"Maybe I should have married that plantation guy my father wanted me to marry. Between Normal School and our rehearsals which run late every night I'm totally exhausted. And my parents are beginning to wonder why the laundry keeps us so late."

"Laundry?" Ito asked.

"Oh, it's all Kimi's fault," Felice accused me. "We knew our parents would never put up with us dancing hula publicly so she suggested we tell them we were working afternoons with her grandmother at a local laundry to earn our school fees. So far it's worked but I don't know for how much longer."

"Poor Felice-san," Ito sympathised. "Your parents sound just like mine. My parents have no idea I'm playing ukelele and helping with the choreography for Emory-san's review. They think I'm working long hours at the university."

"Teri'i tink dat wat Felice need is few days off and go Kauai wit Ito and Teri'i. How bout it? Once boss Emory satisfied revue all right den we get days off. Dat wat he say, anyway."

I felt really irritated. Teri'i and Ito had managed to convince Felice that her life wasn't complete without seeing the sights on Kauai and I knew that neither of us had time to do that. Unless we used every minute free of rehearsal to do our assignments we would never achieve the grades that would allow us to be teachers on Oahu. Only the best were selected for Oahu and the others had to teach in rural areas.

"Felice," I complained. "You're going to wind up teaching in some remote place like Waipio Valley if you go off joy riding with Ito and Teri'i. You know how hard it is to convince school boards that Hawaiian and Portuguese teachers can teach in predominently white areas like Honolulu."

"Forget Normal School, Felice," Teri'i ordered. "Dat why Teri'i and Ito never see Kimi and Felice during day?"

"Felice and I have spent the last six years doing nothing else but preparing ourselves to become teachers. We can't just throw all we have accomplished away."

"No be teachers, Kimi! Teri'i tell you befo. Teachers be old maids. Tahitian dancers make it beeg." I was startled by the emotion in Teri'i's voice.

"You dancers, singers, entertainers, just like Teri'i, Ito," he insisted. "Crowd love Polynesian Revue! Become beeg stars. Stay show business all life. Have fun, laugh, sing. Always happy. Maybe even be famous some day. Rich men chase all time. Wan marry lovely ladies. Teacher be old maid. Job hard. Put Hawaiian students down. Mark all time. Pay nothing."

I gasped. I'd thought of nothing for the last five years than becoming a teacher.

"Maybe Teri'i's right, Kimi." I couldn't believe Felice's words.

"There's sure not much laughter in our classes. Dr. Curtis, our Principal, is so serious. Always telling us how we have to maintain standards. Telling us how employers expect proper work attitudes from our students when they graduate. And perfect spoken and written English. Even though it's only the Haole students that speak English out of school. And Dr. Curtis marks so hard. Even for the slightest mistake."

"And the statistics Dr. Curtis told us about the other day. Imagine, twenty percent of students in Hawaii don't even get to go on to Grade Eight. They fail the English grammar exam. What happens to those students?"

"Oh, they're just Hawaiian, Filipino and Portuguese students who aren't being taught properly, Felice. It will be different when we teach them, I'm sure."

"Besides Dr. Curtis is just trying to increase our level of dedication to the teaching profession."

"You too serious, Kimi," Teri'i complained. "My family, in Tahiti, say play OK, too."

"Don't be silly Teri'i," I protested. "You don't know how hard Felice and I worked to get accepted into Normal School. It's the best thing that ever happened to us. It'll give us the means to have a better life than our parents." Teri'i's words were really upsetting me. I tried to explain.

"We just work for the Tropical Palace as dancers to pay our school fees. Once we get our teacher certification we won't be in show business any longer."

"Teri'i sad, Kimi. Miss you and Felice."

I started. Teri'i's voice had real pain in it.

"I didn't think he thought that much of me," I caught myself thinking. That thought caused an odd feeling in my heart.

"Don't be silly, Kimi Kai`ika," I mentally warned myself. "Don't you go falling for some big hulk, no matter how good looking and sweet he is. Why Teri'i will never be anything but a fire dancer." Then I looked at his face. He looked so earnest I couldn't bring myself to put him down like I knew I should.

"How sweet of you Teri'i," I surprised myself by saying. Then I grabbed onto my emotions.

"Why, I'm sure Felice and I will miss you too. After all the time we've spent rehearsing, of course."

"Maybe you try teach Teri'i, read, write? English better now. Den Teri'i still see you."

My heart seemed to react violently again.

"Why, the poor guy. He's even willing to learn to read and write to still see me," I thought.

"Sure Teri'i, I'll help you learn to read and write," I found myself blurting. Then I managed to steel myself a little again.

"Haven't you given Teri'i any help, Ito. I know you go to the University of Hawaii, too. Can't you show Teri'i how to read?"

"I have tried, Kimi," Ito replied, becoming uncharacteristically serious. "I tried instructing him. particularly trying to get Teri'i-san to read sheet music. But I think he's got some kind of handicap or something. Teri'i-san seems to read from right to left, instead of left to right, no matter what I do. Maybe you could take a look at his reading Kimi? With your teacher training maybe you could find out why he's having so much trouble."

"We won't be finished Normal School for close to a year, anyway," I returned to rationality. "Felice and I still have a ten months practicum to complete. I guess I could try to help Teri'i learn to read and write."

"Kimi teach Teri'i read?" His voice was really excited. "Den Teri'i pay Kimi back. Teach Kimi how drive Teri'i's new car."

"You bought a new car?"

"Yes Kimi. But not new, used. Pay check only allow down payment fo used car. But good shape."

Teri'i's offer tempted me. I had always wanted to learn to drive but Mother wouldn't let us drive her old car.

"You've got a deal, Teri'i." I agreed. "I'll teach you to read and you can teach me driving."

"Come early rehearsal, Kimi. Every day one hour befo."

"Time to go back now," Felice sighed. "Mr. Emory is waving frantically from the ballroom. My poor feet. That beat we're dancing to is fierce."

We made our way back into the ballroom.

"Teri'i, can you sing?" I was astonished to hear Mr. Emory ask.

"Sure, Boss, Teri'i sing church choir Papeete."

"Then, learn these lyrics. It's a new song I've written just for the revue. I want you to sing it to Kimi on top of Haleakala when you find the Silversword plant."

"Kimi," Teri'i whispered to me. "You read song out loud

quick?" Some of the entertainers picked up what Teri'i was saying. They looked at him with shock.

"Sure Teri'i," I answered. My heart was aching again. I could feel Teri'i's shame at not being able to read. We went out into the hallway area and I read the lyrics to him a few times. Teri'i was amazing. Within minutes he had memorized every line.

"Where did you get such a good memory?" I asked.

"No choice, Kimi. I no able read in school. Get called stupid. Run away. But learn memorize words in church choir. Not wan be kicked out."

"OK, Boss. I know words." We returned to Mr. Emory. "How music go?"

"Take Ito and go over to the lounge, Teri'i. The piano player will play the tune for you and Ito. I want Ito to play this song on his ukelele as you sing it to Kimi. There's a singing instructor to teach you to use your lungs more when you sing, too. She's waiting in the lounge."

"Felice, look alive, I want you to practice that Latin American congo line for me again. It went over well with the lounge customers last night. I want to include it the opening night of the revue."

"Kimi," I started as Mr. Emory addressed me.

"Go over to Housekeeping. I've designed a white gown for you for one of my new numbers. The housekeeper needs your measurements."

"OK, dancers, let's go over that routine again. First trumpet, come in a little sooner, keep your eye on my baton at all times."

And so it went until the night of the opening. The Hotel was frantic. I knew that hundreds of tourists had descended on the Tropical Palace and the other two hotels with the arrival of the Malolo in Honolulu Harbor the night before.

It looked to me that our boss had become a nervous wreck. He was still dictating finishing touches to the costumes and stage sets. The final rehearsal had been a disaster. Some of the singers were still blowing their lines. I couldn't help laughing at the rehearsal when one of our dance troupe resembled a football lineback charging through to the head of the line. He had panicked completely when he forgot the steps to the intricate dance up the side of Haleakala.

"I'll be the laughing stock of show business," I heard Mr. Emory say to the bartender as the long hours must have caught up to him.

"Have a Zombie, Mr. Emory," the bartender told him. "It'll still your nerves. Don't worry. Remember the words in one of our songs. Something like, in Hawaii we never fret, we never worry."

"Maybe Hawaiians don't, but what about Haoles? It's Haoles that I have to satisfy, not Hawaiians."

"Don't be too sure, Mr. Emory. I understand Hawaii's Delegate to Congress who's a Hawaiian, and some of the leading citizens of the Hawaiian community will be at the head table tomorrow night along with the Board of Directors of the Tropical Palace Hotel."

"Oh, my God! Let me know when my new tuxedo comes back, will you? That fool of a tailor cut the pants six inches too short. He promised to fix them but I can only hope he can make good on his promise."

"Oh, that must be why there's a guy over in Housekeeping trying to steam a pair of pants longer."

"Good Lord, what if they shrink during the performance? God knows I usually sweat a quart of liquid during a show."

I went home feeling pretty nervous.

"No worry, Kimi," Tutu said. "Remember, you only after money fo school fees. No going be Tahitian dancer all life, particularly if mother find out. Tutu worried. Maybe someone who know Kimi see opening."

"I hope not, Tutu," I laughed. She was right. I wasn't going to be a Tahitian dancer all my life. What did I care what happened to the revue. Felice and I just needed it for ten more months anyway.

"But what if Tutu is right and someone sees the opening that knows me and my mother," I worried. "Or someone who knows Felice and her family. They still think we work at the laundry for the afternoon shift."

Then I put such thoughts out of my mind.

"What would poor people like those who know Felice's and my families be doing at the Tropical Palace Hotel?" I reasoned.

Chapter 10.

Opening Night.

Atherton Scully felt cautiously optimistic as he sat waiting for his wife and Norman Baker at the head table of the ballroom. He was waiting for all the invited guests to show before he could give the signal to Winston Emory to start the proceedings. Atherton realised he had been at the hotel without a day off for the last fifty days.

"Jessica complains she never sees me anymore," I sighed. "And God knows it was my idea to buy into this hotel. Jessica's sure seeing a lot of Norman Baker, though, lately. He even insisted on her accompanying him to the opening. I wonder if they could be having an affair?"

"How ridiculous," I told myself. "Why Norman's as old as Jessica's father would be. I must be developing Paranoia. "

I breathed a sigh of relief as I spotted Norman and Jessica entering the heavily decorated Ballroom. They sat down next to me and I gave the signal to Winston Emory to begin his new music medley. Emory picked up his baton and the hotel orchestra broke into a piece that sounded familiar. Hawaiian warriors came out of the back of the stage and pretended a mock battle with each other all the time being careful to maintain the fast rhythm of the piece. Winston Emory had done something spectacular to the piece. Brass had been added and the rhythm was much easier to listen to. Anxiously I scanned the faces of our specially invited guests to guage their reaction to the new sound. Everyone was listening intently. I sighed with relief as the Delegate to Congress nodded with approval.

"Thank God, the guests seem to love the new rhythm," I said to Jessica as I realised most of the guests were looking entranced.

"The new revue is wonderful so far, Dear," Jessica replied.

"Indeed, Atherton," Norman Baker added his stamp of approval. I started to feel really pleased as the all important passengers off the Malolo clapped loudly. "It's unbelievable what Winston Emory has done to the old tunes, Atherton," Jessica said at the first break. "Why, Emory's given the old tunes new life and a rhythm that can be danced to. It's such a transformation."

I watched the audience closely again as the stage curtains opened to reveal a replica of the Haleakala Volcano crater. Emory's dancers went into their routines. The audience was completely absorbed in the action. I spotted Hawaii's Delegate to Congress. He was wiping tears from his eyes as the history of the first Polynesians arriving on Maui was portrayed. I glanced at the ladies as Prince Teri'i started his seranade to Kimi Kai'ika on top of Haleakala. The wives of the wealthy businessmen from the Malolo looked like their hearts had been captured forever. At the end of the the Maui number the audience applauded thunderously.

After another short break I watched as Emory's two hula girls, Kimi Kai'ika and Felice did the Tahitian Tamure. I quickly realised they were capturing the undivided attention of every wealthy stockbroker in the Ballroom with their spirited interpretation.

I looked closely at Norman Baker and Jessica as Alan Carstairs took the stage. They both watched intently. I smiled to myself when Jessica broke into tears as he sang one of Emory's creations, a new love song entitled 'Under The Tropical Moon,' while Kimi Kai`ika danced to it.

At another intermission I listened to what the invited

newspaper critics had to say. I glowed as they gave Winston Emory top marks for his Hawaiian arrangements.

I was about to order a round of champagne to celebrate when one of our table members got into an argument with Jessica. I glanced over and recognised an old friend of mine, Iwana Keaka. The old fellow was a coutier from King Kalakau's time and was very respected in the Hawaiian community. Conversation went dead as he and Jessica got into a shouting match.

"How dare you question what Winston Emory is doing to the old Island music?" Jessica yelled at Iwana. I nearly died of embarrassment. When Jessica lost her temper she went into a blind rage.

"It's paradoxical, you know," Iwana announced to the entire head table with an infuriating air of superiority. "What your Music Director and the other ones at the other Hotels have done to our old music has made it enchanting to western ears. I foresee those young fellows giving years of pleasure to visitors to Hawaii. And yet their music is another nail in the coffin of Hawaiian culture. Their lyrics are insulting to Hawaiians, both kanes and wahines, and their dance routines take our sacred hula and oral history and transform them into a Hollywood plot and chorus line."

Jessica choked on her champagne at his words. Her face turned a bright shade of red. I could see that Iwana's remarks were triggering her.

"How dare you criticize what our wonderful Music Director has done to that old pagan, monotonous chanting directed to idols? Why, what Winston Emory has done has taken music not fit for human ears and transformed it into an aesthetic masterpiece."

"Just listen to some of the lyrics that Emory has borrowed from one of the other hotels, Mrs. Scully," Iwana ignored the rage evident in Jessica's voice, eyes, and body posture. "If you ask me, our Hawaiian hotels and radio stations put too much stock in what mainland Haoles value."

"Princess Poopooly Has Plenty Papayas," is promoting

Hawaiian wahines breast sizes," Iwana continued his attack. "Okele maluna' (Bottoms Up), is promoting alcohol consumption. And the fragile white gowns in 'Under The Tropical Moon,' will undoubtedly stimulate the garment industry but in manufacturing American-style dresses instead of Hawaiian."

"What are you saying, Iwana?" Hawaii's Delegate to Congress gasped. "Hapa-haole music has always been a great boon to the tourist industry here in Hawaii."

"Oh, My God," I thought. "All we need is an angry debate reported in the Sunday newspaper. And I'm the one who invited Iwana to the opening. I'm sure Jessica will want a divorce if she finds out I did that." I realised I had a big pilikia on my hands.

Norman Baker was making frantic hand gestures to me to do something about Iwana.

"Winston Emory is distorting our history, selling our young people as sex objects, and giving a completely western sound to our sacred chants. The tourist and development boom that Emory's music will spawn will result in even more land being removed from Indigenous Hawaiians. The few native families managing to cling to land these days are threatened again."

Jessica went into a coughing spasm at Iwana's latest words.

"How dare you criticize the music in this Ballroom?" she choked. "And the Tourist Industry in Hawaii in the presence of our invited guests?"

My heart nearly stopped as a distinguished music student of former Queen Lili'uokalani raised his voice and joined the debate.

"Iwana is right. Hawaiian songs should be sung only in the Hawaiian language," he insisted. "And in the proper tempo they were composed in. Why your Music Director has Orientalized popular Hawaiian pieces dating back all the way into the late 18th. Century."

"What an insult to the popular hapa-haole music that Emory had devised," I thought. Jessica went into a full blown rage.

"Pre-contact Hawaiian music promoted promiscuity and was

dedicated to pagan idols," she shouted. The hula was only luring a sinful people into promiscuity. Thank Heavens a more advanced race was able to still such barbaric heathenism." I realised Jessica was echoing the belief system of her dead father.

"Just listen to those lyrics your Music Director has borrowed, Mrs. Scully," Iwana chimed in again.

"Hawaii, a land of make-believe, come true." Maybe for Haoles, all right, living in luxury on beach-front properties. But what about the poor, Indigenous Hawaiians living in hovels up in the mountains. Haole's have taken everything we used to own and now they're expropriating our music and culture for tourism and real estate development as well. They are turning our culture and young wahines into a commodity that can be sold."

"Saying we do nothing but dance and sing all day to lure tourists to Paradise. Paraphrasing the lyrics, Mrs. Scully, 'Hawaiians never worry, they never fret, just laze in the sun all day long.' What kind of message is that to Hawaii's youth?"

"Iwana, you're being absurd," I tried to get the old boy to stop. "Just because Winston Emory has given Hawaiian music harmony, rhythm and romance. Why, I predict these songs will be big hits in Hollywood. Tourists will be drawn like flies to Hawaii from destinations everywhere."

"Mark my words, Keaka," Norman Baker agreed with me. "Atherton is right. The Tourist Industry will replace sugar as the leading industry in Hawaii. The enlightenment evident in our Islands will make us a shining beacon to the rest of the world."

"How wonderful," Iwana sarcastically exclaimed.

The Maitre D had finally responded to my frantic hand signals.

"Remove Mr. Keaka from the Ballroom," I ordered. "I'm afraid he's had too much of the alcoholic punch." Iwana got in a few more words shouted across the Ballroom as the Maitre D dragged him out.

"And what will happen when there isn't enough land to build accomodations for those myriads of tourists or resources to feed them. When resources are needed for tourism and housing for the thousands of mainlanders flocking to paradise, who will win, big business or indigenous Hawaiians."

"Don't be ridiculous, Iwana," I yelled at his retreating back. "There will always be enough resources for everyone here in Paradise."

"My apologies, Ladies and Gentleman. An embittered ali'i." I poured oil on troubled waters as Winston Emory resumed the entertainment.

"Waiter, another round of champagne," I ordered.

The second half of the medley went without any more adverse publicity. It was extremely well received by the audience. I returned home and spent several hours trying to calm Jessica down.

The next morning I scanned the Sunday paper anxiously to see if Iwana's outburst had been reported.

"Fortunately the paper haven't reported anything about the debate at the head table," I said to Jessica as I skimmed the news.

"Whatever possessed you to invite that senile Kanaka?"

I winced as Jessica's temper started flaring again.

I was saved by the telephone. It was Norman Baker.

"Congratulations," I relaxed as Baker's voice was as pleasant as I had ever heard it.

"The members of the Board wanted me to relay to you how pleased we are with your management of the Hotel. The hotels clients are saying only glowing things about their rooms and hotel services. And the papers are calling the new revue a great success. Winston Emory's themes are just what I'd hoped them to be. I've been in touch with some friends of mine and there's another conference on Hawaii's role in International politics being scheduled for the end of the year."

"On another matter, Atherton, it's so good of you to let me use Jessica as my official hostess at my dinner parties. I'd like to thank you so much for that."

"My pleasure, Norman," I responded. "God knows I haven't

the time I used to to spend with her in the evenings. I owe you my thanks for keeping her occupied."

"Then you won't mind my taking her to Maui for the annual business meeting of Aquanar, one of my businesses next month, Atherton. I do so need a hostess for the event."

"Certainly, Norman," I replied.

"Darling, Norman Baker wants you to be his hostess for one of his annual Business meetings in Maui." I covered the mouthpiece.

"I realise it will be pretty boring for you but would you do it for the old boy anyway. As I favor to me," I begged.

Jessica's look of anger disappeared. A pleased smile came to her face and she nodded affirmatively.

"Maybe she'll be less demanding of my time if she thinks she's doing something useful for Baker," I thought.

Chapter 11.

Repercussions.

"Look at the newspaper, Kimi," I heard Felice shout as she burst into our kitchen waving the Sunday paper. I was sitting with Tutu having breakfast. Mother and Kimo had gone to the Sunday service. I was so tired from last night's show and the party afterwards to celebrate. It had gone on into the late hours of the morning.

"Kimi, the music critic says that the opening of our revue last night was an unprecedented success. And look what he says about you and I."

"Adding to the freshness and vitality of the new Tropical Palace revue is the heart-throbbing rhythm of the Tahitian Tamure. This dance was aided immensely by the charm of two of the Island's most talented dancers, Kimi Kai`ika and Felice Santos."

"Maybe we should give up the idea of becoming teachers like Teri'i says, Kimi. Maybe we have much more of a future in show business. Ito was telling me that Mr. Scully will likely give us big raises thanks to the popularity of our Tahitian Tamure."

I reeled. Tutu looked at me horrified.

"Kimi, names in paper?" Tutu asked. I grabbed the paper out of Felice's hands.

"Oh, God. They do mention us by name." Fear shot through

me. "Felice, our parents are going to have a fit. My mother still thinks we're still working the afternoon shift with Tutu in the laundry. Did you ever have the nerve to tell your father how you're really paying your school fees?"

"God no, Kimi!" Felice's voice had real fear in it as she realised the danger we were in.

"Mother be furious at Tutu," my grandmother said putting both hands over her heart.

"She tink me kipi (traitor) to my husband. Allow old ways be changed for Haoles. And lie to her. Mother never forgive tutu, Kimi."

"Tutu, don't blame yourself," I tried to cheer her up. "You were only trying to help me have a better life."

"My God, we've got to destroy this newspaper," Felice went into a panic.

"Maybe no one from around here will read the entertainment page," I tried to reassure her.

"You don't know my father." Felice's voice was full of terror. "He's going to do something brutal if he finds out I'm dancing in public to fast moving music. Particularly if he sees our costumes."

"Girls, Tutu sorry," Grandmother sobbed. "Never tink tell you use stage names. Beeg pilikia, Kimi. Now your mother and Felice's father get furious, maybe even go crazy."

"All of Oahu is going to know what we're doing before our parents do, Tutu. We're going to have to explain to them fast."

"Not worry bout Mother, Kimi. Tutu speak, explain. She listen, maybe. But not Felice's fadder. Tutu see him go pupule (crazy) befo. Father want Felice be good Portugee daughter. No public life before respectable Portugee marriage. Only let Hawaiian wife send Felice to hula lessons because sacred hula not public. Father hear Felice dance coconut shell. He go pupule. Lock Felice away. Hotel job pau (gone.)"

"Tutu," I protested. "We can't quit now." I agonized. We've still got ten months to go before we graduate. Maybe no one who knows us will read the Entertainment section."

Just then the phone on the wall rang shrilly. I picked it up, my heart beating wildly.

"Aloha," I tried to keep my voice from showing the fear I felt. Then I recognized our kumu hula's voice. I went white.

"Tutu, it's Aunt Auhea," I gasped.

"Yes, the newspaper is correct," I croaked as her angry accusation deadened my eardrums. "But I can explain."

Klunk. The receiver was slammed in my ear. I broke into tears.

"She'll go right to mother and complain, Tutu, I know it," I sobbed.

"Kimi right. She be on way Church now."

"We've got to tell Felice's parents first, Tutu, before Aunt Auhea does."

I phoned over to Felice's. The line was busy.

"It's busy, Tutu," I sighed.

"No time, Kimi. Too late already. Aunt Auhea talk Mr. Santos. Tutu tink fast."

"We'll have to quit, Kimi." I had never heard Felice sound so scared. "My father is going to beat me, I know it."

"Your father has no right to beat you. You're an adult now."

"That won't stop him. We had better go right to the hotel and quit. That might at least save me from scars. You have no idea how unreasonable my father can be."

"No. We can't do that. Our lives will be nothing if we don't make it through Normal School this year. I understand the teaching program is being switched over to the University of Hawaii soon. We'll never be able to afford it if it's moved up to a four year program like the University wants."

"Kimi," Tutu's voice sounded urgent. "Pack clothes wiki wiki. Take Felice. Go. Somewhere parents no look for Felice."

"But Tutu, we can't just run away."

"Do what Tutu order, Kimi. I talk your Mother. She likely OK but no can handle Felice's Father. Tutu know. Talk Felice's mother once. She black and blue from beating. Felice father he go pupule."

"Maybe you're right, Tutu." I'd seen bruises on Felice when Mr. Santos had been displeased before. I ran to the bedroom and threw some clothes into a laundry bag.

"It too late, Kimi, Felice screamed." I heard a car screech to a halt in front of the house. The front door slammed open.

"Felice, where are you?" shouted Mr. Santos. He was all alone.

Felice burst into tears.

"I can explain, Mr. Santos," I tried.

He glared at me and went over and slapped Felice viciously across the face with his hand. She screamed and fell backwards into the wall.

"Go to car, Felice," Mr. Santos shouted. "You shame family. Dance lewd in public." He pushed Felice towards the door.

"Don't go Felice," I shouted. I moved between Felice and her father. I knew I had to stop Felice from getting into the car with him.

"Mr. Santos. Felice and I are adults. You've no right to tell us what to do." I could see Mr. Santos eyes go funny. He lunged at me and grabbed me with both hands.

"This your fault, Kimi. You bad example for Felice." He shook me hard. "No obey Mother. Lie. I punish fo her." Mr. Santos raised his hand to strike me. I cringed.

"No touch Kimi or Felice," Tutu charged in between Mr. Santos and I. She had the heavy cast iron frying pan from the stove in her hand. I backed towards Felice and the door.

Mr. Santos laughed.

"Wat you do wit pan, old woman," he growled. "Your fault, too, Felice shame family. Aunt Auhea tell truth."

Mr. Santos advanced towards Tutu and grabbed the pan out of her hand. He threw the pan across the room. It hit the wall beside Felice and myself with a crash.

"Now what you do, old lady?" He struck Tutu on the face. She fell backwards to the floor. I grabbed the frying pan.

"Stay away from Tutu, Mr. Santos," I warned.

He started towards me uttering a sharp growl. I hit him as hard as I could on the head. He slumped to his knees. I hit him again. He dropped to the floor.

"Kimi, no hit again," Tutu warned. "Might kill."

"We've got to get out of here, Tutu, before he comes to," I shouted. I helped her get up off the floor. She had a bad bruise across her right cheek. I knew we had to find someone stronger than Mr. Santos fast. Then it came to me.

"We can run to Teri'i's place, Felice. He's moved out of Ito's and rented a tenement. He'll protect us. Besides, Teri'i bought that old car with his paychecks. He'll help us find a place to stay."

"Kimi," Felice was crying. "I can't run away. I'll never see my mother or sisters again."

"He'll beat you. You know it. And he'll make you marry that older plantation worker he's got picked out for you. It's your whole life you're talking about here."

"Go, Kimi," Tutu warned. "No time. Take clothes. No come back for awhile. Till Felice father go back normal."

"Tutu, I'm not going to let you stay here until Mr. Santos regains consciousness. You've got to get out of here, too."

"I run to church, Kimi. Tell mother what happened."

"We'll take Mr. Santos's car. That way he can't come after us." I reached in Mr. Santos's pocket and found his car keys. He groaned on the floor.

I grabbed some clothes and threw them into a bag. Then I seized Felice's hand and dragged her out the door. Tutu came out of the house, too. We rushed over to Mr. Santos' car. We put the clothes in the back seat. Tutu climbed in.

"Kimi, how you know drive?"

"Teri'i showed me. In exchange for me trying to help him read."

I started the car, threw it into gear and roared out the road. I went straight to our church and parked in the parking lot. I didn't have the courage to face my mother yet but I knew we had to leave the car at the church or Mr. Santos would claim I stole it.

"You tell mother, Tutu. She can drive you back and see how Mr. Santos is. I'll take Felice to Teri'i's place. It isn't very far from here. He'll help us, I know it."

We picked up the clothes from the back seat.

"This is our chance. Tutu's gone into the church. The service is just about over. Tutu will tell mother and they can check on your father. We better be miles away from here before he finds us. We dragged the bag of clothes between the two of us.

It seemed like we walked for miles in fear that the police or someone would come down the road. Fortunately Teri'i didn't live too far away.

"Teri'i, open up," I yelled as we came to the door of his tenement building. I gave thanks to God when I saw his car was out front and I knew he was home.

"Kimi, Felice, wat you do here?" Teri'i looked completely shocked. We charged in and sat down on Teri'i's old kitchen furniture.

"Place not much," he apologised. "But car more important," he beamed. His smile stopped suddenly as he saw Felice in tears. He spotted the bruise on Felice's face where Mr. Santos had struck her.

"Why Felice hurt?" he demanded.

"It's a disaster," I told him quickly. I blurted out what had happened.

"Felice never told her parents we are dancing in a hula troupe. They wouldn't have allowed it. My mother and Felice's parents thought we were working the afternoon shift at my grandmother's laundry. Now the newspaper has published our names in the revue of the show. Our hula kumu saw it and told Felice's father. He went berserk. He struck Felice and I swear he would have choked me if I hadn't hit him with a frying pan. I don't know what he's going to do if he finds either one of us."

"Kimi hit Felice fadder wit frying pan?" Teri'i looked amazed.

"He was going to hurt Tutu," I explained.
"No worry, Felice. Teri'i stop Father. You safe here."
"Thanks, you're wonderful," I told him. I could feel my heart throbbing strangely. "Teri'i is always so understanding," I thought. "Just like Tutu."
"We need you to drive us around to see if Felice and I can find a room for rent. We're going to have to hide out for awhile."
"Top floor room fo rent here. Better den dis room, but landlord want mo money. Teri'i help if fadder come."
"Thanks, Teri'i!" Felice looked slightly relieved. She wiped her tears with a hankerchief.
"You'll have to stay here with me, Kimi, if you want me to keep on dancing. I'm not going to live alone in this working class part of Honolulu."
"I'll likely have to, anyway," I replied. I realised that my mother was going to be very upset about my dancing anything but the Hula Kahiko. Not to mention my not telling her the truth. And hitting Mr. Santos over the head twice with a frying pan."
"Actually, Tutu is likely to wind up with us here, too," I added.
Teri'i took us over to the landlord's house in his car.
"Mr. Tanaka, dese ladies work wit me at Tropical Palace Hotel. Want rent room on top floor." Mr. Tanaka eyed us warily.
"No party, no male visitors, no pets, no radio. Rent ten dollars in advance," he warned.
"Teri'i," I whispered. "I won't have that much money until next payday."
"No pilikia," he beamed. He pulled out a ten dollar bill from his pocket and slipped it to me.
"Saving fo insurance fo car. Felice, Kimi mo important."
"Thank you." I hugged Teri'i. My heart beat seemed to pick up speed as I did so. "He's so sweet," I found myself thinking gratefully. My heart was doing flip-flops again.
"You've saved our lives."
"No franternizing with other tentants in house," Mr. Tankaa warned as I hugged Teri'i again. "House have good reputation."

I gave Mr. Tanaka the ten dollar bill. He handed me a key. "Supply own bedding and dishes," he instructed. "I speak Boss Emory, Kimi. Tell him your pilikia. Felice fadder might turn up Hotel. Need security look-out fo him."

"Thanks. You're right. Thank Heavens we're on a break from Normal School." I hugged him again.

"I don't know if I can go through with this." Felice was having second thoughts. "It's going to be so lonely without my family."

"You don't have any choice. You'll miss them anyway if you have to relocate with that plantation worker your father wants you to marry. That's if you don't have every bone in your body broken first."

"Don't even think such a thing." Felice sobbed. We arrived back at the tenement.

I opened the door cautiously, expecting a terrible mess. However, the room didn't look as bad as I'd expected. It was clean and livable. It had a double bed and a kitchen table and chairs. And like Mr. Tanaka said," I remembered. "House have good reputation."

"It'll all be worth it someday." Felice dissolved in tears on the bed.

The next afternoon when we reported to the Tropical Palace the receptionists told us that Mr. Scully wanted to see us in his office. When Felice and I entered my heart nearly stopped.

A parish priest was seated in the office in one of Mr. Scully's big chairs.

"Felice Santos," the priest said sharply. "I must warn you that your immortal soul is in danger if you insist on continuing on with your present job." Felice looked like a scared little girl.

"These young ladies are under contract, Father Julius," Mr. Scully interrupted. "Our revue can't possibly continue without them. They are simply irreplaceable."

"Felice," Father Julius's voice ordered. "Your father wants you to return home with me now. He's arranged for you to marry

Julio Pasquello, an honorable plantation worker a few years your senior. I assure you this is the correct thing to do."

"Never, Father," Felice found the courage to answer. "I'd rather die. Julio Pasquello is twice my age."

"Then I'm afraid I have no choice but to remove your name from our roll of parishioners," he threatened.

I gasped. I realised he was threatening to excommunicate Felice from the Church.

"Your father wishes for me to tell you that you are to come home now or you will no longer have a home."

"I'm sorry, Father. I can't marry Julio Pasquello," Felice sobbed.

"You have the rest of the day to think about this and contact me."

Father Julius nodded to Atherton Scully and left the room. He looked furious.

"I'm so embarrassed, Mr. Scully," Felice stammered.

"Please don't be, Miss Santos. Believe me I understand how difficult these family situations can be. Don't hesitate to ask if you need my help in any way. But remember. Both you girls are adults. You're entitled to make your own decisions."

"By the way," Mr. Scully added as we started to leave.

"Winston Emory has requested that I give both you young ladies a raise. He says you're the stars of the show, along with Prince Teri'i and Alan Carstairs, of course. I couldn't agree more. Consider your salaries doubled. Just sign these contracts for me."

Felice and I signed without even reading what we were signing.

"Thank you Mr. Scully." I managed for both of us. I realised Felice and I could meet our expenses now as well as our school fees.

"Take the rest of the day off if you need it," Mr. Scully advised.

Felice went back to our rented room to sort out her thoughts. I went to the laundry to tell Tutu what had happened.

My heart nearly stopped as I opened the door and saw my mother waiting with Tutu."

I stared at my mother closely. She was looking very sad, with tears coming down her cheeks.

"Kimi, how could you have done dis?" she asked. "Become a kipi (traitor) to sacred hula and causing all dis trouble for Felice."

"Mother," I gasped. "Can't you let me tell my side of the story?" I stared hard at her. She looked so old and tired.

"All her years of hard labor and scrounging materials for leis to sell on the waterfront day and night are taking their toll," I thought.

"I'm not going to let that happen to me," I vowed. I tried to strengthen my resolve. I knew my mother was going to try and get me to quit.

"Felice and I don't have any choice," I told myself. "I'm going to wind up burned out like my mother and Felice is going to wind up oppressed with a husband she doesn't love if we give in." I braced myself for the words I knew were coming.

"Your side? Nothing to tell. You lie, betray Hula Kahiko secrets in public, and make laughingstock of old ways."

"What are you talking about? All Felice and I did was find a way to pay our fees for Normal School. I'm sorry I didn't tell you but I knew you wouldn't understand."

"Kimi, no yell," Tutu interrupted. I realised I was shouting at the top of my voice.

"You two try listen each udder. Clash. Old ways wit new. Kimi, Mother wan you follow old ways. Mother, Kimi wan you let her have better life dan grow taro in Waipio Valley."

"Try be patient with Mother, Kimi. She very huhu."

"I can't be patient any longer," I sobbed. Anger and resentment seemed to be filling my mind. I couldn't imagine living in the remote Waipio Valley on the Big Island of Hawaii. It was even more cut off than Nanakuli where we had been brought up until moving to the city.

"Mother, you have to understand," I shouted. "I want to be a teacher and help Hawaiian students get through High School so they can do something with their lives."

"Kimi," my mother spoke sharply. "Kanakas never get to High School. Why you tink English grammar test brought in. Aunt Auhea explain. Test stop Kanakas from go to good Haole schools, even if live next door. Haoles want Kanakas be servants, dock workers, plantation workers, beach boys."

I didn't believe my mother. "More Aunt Auhea propaganda," I thought.

"Perhaps more Kanakas would pass the exam if I taught them, Mother."

"Kimi, you hupo (fool). Kanakas have no chance. Even if you pass teacher school, there be no job for you in City. Haole teachers hired first, or Chinese, Japanese maybe, if all positions not filled."

"There's some Hawaiian teachers, Mother," I shouted.

"Only rural schools. Hanapepe, Hilo. And den only if no Haole teacher willing go there."

"What are you saying, Mother?" My head reeled.

"She's been brainwashed by Aunt Auhea," I thought. I refused to believe what she was saying.

"Discrimination, Kimi. Haoles make sure only Haoles get professional jobs. Kanakas good only for servants and dock workers in dere minds."

"That can't be true," I shouted.

"You hupo, Kimi. Tink you beat discrimination. No way. You no understand Haole rules. Come home now. Give up idea of dancing hula fo money. Even if you get trough teaching school, dere be no jobs. You see. Waste money go teacher training. No way beat Haole discrimination."

"How can you know that?" I shouted.

"I try Kimi. Study for years be practical nurse befo marry. Graduate but no jobs in hospital. Only Haoles hired. I finally understand. Go wit your father to Nanakuli. We have enough of Haole ways."

Tears came to my eyes. I didn't want to believe what my mother was telling me.

"You work Laundry with Tutu, Kimi. We save, go Waipio, grow taro. Or maybe Hilo, grow orchids. Sell leis. Live in old way. Den Haoles no control. Grow own food. Fish. Not have be servant or slave on plantation."

"No, Mother," I shouted. "This is a new time era. It might have been like that for you but it won't be for me." My head was whirling. I felt choked. I didn't want to believe her. Why hadn't she told me about trying to be a nurse before.

"Why should I give up everything I've worked for so hard for so long. If I don't become a teacher I'll never have any kind of life at all," I yelled.

"Kimi, you no be teacher anyway. I know. You see. I wait till you come to senses."

Mother went towards the door. I realised all of Tutu's workmates were staring at us in horror.

"Then I'll stay in show business," I yelled at my mother totally choked with disbelief. "At least show business pays more than laundry wages," I shouted.

"Kimi, you sell out old ways," my mother turned and said sadly. "Comic hula you dance shame sacred hula. Songs you and Felice sing tell of Haole romance. Oppress Hawaiian wahines. Sell bodies for Haole money. Songs not Hawaiian. Written Tin Pan Alley, and Hollywood."

"I save money from lei selling, Kimi. Buy land in Waipio or Hilo. Take Kimo and grow taro or orchids. You join when come senses."

Mother went through the laundry doorway. She closed the door firmly. I could hear our old car start up in the driveway, idle for a few minutes and then drive off. Tears surged down my face.

"Kimi, geev Mother time," Tutu pleaded. She held me close. I cried hysterically in her bosom.

"She no understand. Tutu speak to her. You come home next week. Maybe Mother change mind."

"Tutu, I'm so tired of doing what she wants," I confessed. "Surely I have a right to do something for myself."

"Maybe mother right?" Tutu said. I stared at her in horror. "Tutu remember. Mother struggle find job as nurse fo years. I thought it just times. No jobs fo anyone. But maybe she right. No teacher or nurse jobs fo Hawaiians. I never see Hawaiian teacher, lawyer, doctor. Only Haole and Oriental."

"Don't be ridiculous Tutu," I shouted. "It's only because Kanakas never pass the English standard exam to go on to High School and College or University. I'll get to be a teacher here on Oahu. You'll see." I forced mother's and tutu's warnings out of my head.

"They can't be right," I thought. "I've worked so hard."

"What happened to Mr. Santos?" I changed the subject.

"Minister call Priest wen I tell him how Mr. Santos strike Felice and Tutu, Kimi."

"Priest come house. Mr. Santos Ok but dizzy. Priest ask Mr. Santos to let him handle matter, Kimi. But don't let Felice visit parents. Mr. Santos still pupule. Might do somting he regret."

"Thanks Tutu. Are you all right?"

"Tutu manage. Maybe you right in long run. Should have life you want. Hawaiians need listen Aloha within. Heart tell them dem wat dey really want. That what dey need do. Maybe Mother wrong."

I went home and told Felice the latest developments.

"God! Can't any of us younger generation Hawaiians get along with our parents? But what if your mother is right? We'll never get teacher positions even if we do struggle through Normal School."

"Don't be silly. Of course we'll get jobs here on Oahu after we get teacher certification."

"I hope you're right, Kimi."

Chapter 12.

Hotel Bookings Slow.

Jessica Scully smiled happily as she sat in Norman Baker's office listening to his voice on his telephone. "Norman and I have grown so close this past year and a half," she thought. "He's the man I thought I married in Atherton. A talented leader with high achievment drive." Norman was on the phone giving some well-needed direction to Atherton.

"Why if it wasn't for Norman," I reasoned, "my husband would be losing the fortune I have invested in the Tropical Palace Hotel."

"Atherton, the board is not happy with the occupancy rate for the past six months. The hotel started out all right following the initial voyage of the Malolo but lately we seem to be going downhill instead of upwards."

I imagined Atherton wincing at the end of the line. He had such an ego problem. Atherton couldn't take criticism at all.

"How I could I have thought that Atherton was the answer to my dreams so many years ago," I wondered. "I guess I'll never know," I thought. "If only he could be more like Norman."

"I know you've got the Tropical Palace operating at full efficiency, Atherton," Norman's voice continued. "But all the hotels have got to find some way to draw more guests from the mainland. Competition is all right if there's enough customers to go around."

"Norman knows intuitively what has to be done to make the Tropical Palace more viable," I realised. I felt the warmth in my heart that I experienced any time I was in Norman's company. "Everytime I'm with Norman it's like we were meant to be together," I reasoned.

"I know the Tropical Palace is satisfying it's guests all right," Norman said patiently as if addressing someone who took a little longer than normal to understand.

"Those questionnaires we request guests to fill out all suggest that they're more than happy with the accomodations but somehow the message isn't being spread about once they return home."

"I do expect you to do something about it Atherton. Any good hotel director can't just sit still while his rental volume doesn't produce enough income to keep up with expenses."

I cursed under my breath. 'Atherton always has been like that," I thought. "Always whining and blubbering instead of taking command of the situation like a real man. He has absolutely no problem solving ability whatsoever."

"I'm way ahead of you Atherton." I listened as Norman told him that he had arranged through his contacts in office for the Territorial Government to fund a radio program that would be beamed to the mainland from Waikiki. He asked Atherton to alert Winston Emory and the hotel orchestra that they were to be broadcast live to the mainland at any time and to create a pilot radio show for as soon as New Year's Eve. He told him to Have Winston Emory include all the siren songs, the songs that would lure tourists.

"I know they are not prepared," Norman argued with Atherton on the other end of the line. "That's why I'm trying to get you to forewarn them ahead of time. I'm telling you it's absolutely imperative that we draw more tourists to Waikiki. A radio show should be very helpful in this regard. With luck it will become syndicated and be broadcast all over the United States. Maybe even Canada as well." Norman hung up the phone abruptly.

"Great idea Norman," I said. "A radio show broadcast to the mainland. Winston Emory's music is all the rage here on Oahu and now it will be too, on the mainland."

"I'll have to call your husband back when I can muster more patience, My Dear. Has he always been this dense or is this a late development in his life?"

"I've been wondering that myself. Now that I think about it I'm afraid Atherton has always been a ditherer."

"If you don't mind me saying it, you deserve better, Jessica. I'm putting up with Atherton because of you but believe me otherwise I'd eliminate any of my employees who lacked initiative when business appears to be slowing."

"Maybe we'll have to alert Winston Emory, ourselves, Jessica, to crank out some more tunes that will lure tourists to Hawaii. Our research indicates the tourists come here in response to tunes that sing of our beautiful Native women, our sun, sand, hula maidens and swaying palm trees."

"Siren songs."

"Exactly, My Dear."

"Atherton always lacked imagination. I wasn't aware of it for years but I guess my father was always the one who told him what to do. He was just completely lost when father died. But I don't want to take up your time dwelling on my personal problems."

I pulled my mind back to business matters.

"You've been doing research on tourism in Hawaii, Norman?"

"Yes, My Dear. Some sampling of the guests when they're arriving and departing. The responses indicate that Winston Emory's type of Hawaiian music is very popular with mainlanders. We're getting some complaints about the authenticity of the music from locals, mind you, some of the older Hawaiians in the music community, but have Emory ignore their criticisms. Just as long as the music sounds even faintly Hawaiian and echoes the big band trend on the mainland our wealthy clients love it."

"The Tropical Palace isn't in serious trouble, is it? I've sunk in all the money that my father left me."

My heart began to beat furiously. If that money was lost I'd be dependent on Atherton's investments in the other Islands.

"Not just when I'm just realising what shortcomings my husband has," I thought.

"Don't worry." My heart flipped at Norman's smile. It made me sense we were together in some kind of conspiracy.

"I'll keep the Tropical Palace in the black for you. Besides, I've got other plans involving us. Plans that are going to make you wealthy beyond your wildest imagination."

"Whatever do you mean?" My mind went into wild speculation. Norman had been a complete gentleman on the many occasions I'd acted as his official hostess for his business gatherings. But unless I was completely mistaken I sensed more than a daughterly interest in me.

"I'm not going to give you the details, yet, My Dear. Just ask Atherton for me if it's all right for you to accompany me on a business trip to Guatemala in a month. We'll be gone for several weeks. I've got a private yacht chartered for the occasion. What I'm going to propose to you has the potential to change your life forever. That is if you don't lack the courage to take advantage of a winning proposition."

My stomach churned. Norman's words made me sense that incredible changes might be coming.

"Norman, you can't leave me in the dark like this. It all sounds quite mysterious."

"Trust me, My Dear. I assure you that your interests have become very dear to me."

The sudden gentleness in Norman's voice seemed to awaken long-lost feelings in my heart. Tears filled my eyes. Norman smiled and handed me one of his hankerchiefs.

"Leave the details to me," he ordered in an affectionate tone.

"I only hope I can convince Atherton to go along with my plans."

Chapter 13.

Complications.

Mother never did relent. It had been over a year since our argument in the laundry but neither one of us had spoken to the other since that afternoon. I stared at Felice's new batch of Portuguese donuts without holes with horror. I had put on over five pounds thanks to Felice's bakery output and I was getting worried I was going to end up like Tutu. They said Hawaiians of old valued size but I figured they didn't need the weight now that they no longer paddled canoes thousands of miles over the ocean.

"Felice, do you have to do so much baking?" I pleaded.

"It makes me feel better. Baking seems to make up for the void I feel from being separated from my family. Do you realise that it's been over a year since I've seen my mother or sisters?"

"I know. I haven't seen Mother or Kimo either. It's a good thing the Normal School program has been keeping us busy with our practicums as well as our duties at the Tropical Palace."

"Let's take the baking over to Teri'i, Felice. We owe him anyway."

"I know. Imagine him saving our lives by driving us all the way out to Nanakuli and Wahiawa every morning for our school practicum placements. I wonder why Dr. Curtis wouldn't place us in schools closer to Honolulu."

"Dr. Curtis told me to be realistic." A feeling of despair

flooded my heart as I thought again of the words of our Territorial Normal School principal when I had complained about being placed so far out of Honolulu.

"It's for your own good Miss Kai`ika," he told me when I'd protested.

"You and Felice have to realise that the few teachers that we do get from the Hawaiian or Portuguese community are placed in rural areas where there are mainly Hawaiian, Portuguese, or Filipino students. The more the school principals in Nanakuli, Wahiawa and Waianae get to know you ladies the more likely they are to hire you when an opening comes along."

Warning bells seemed to go off in my brain. I remembered my mother's warning the last time she had spoken to me.

"Maybe my mother was right," I allowed myself to admit for a brief moment. "Maybe Felice and I won't find teaching jobs in neighborhoods where there are Haole students like she said."

"But what about Felice, Dr. Curtis?" I asked.

"She's not only Hawaiian, she's half Portuguese."

"That's why I'm placing her in the Catholic School in Wahiawa. Catholic schools are the only ones likely to hire Felice."

"I don't understand."

"Discrimination, Miss Kai'ika, but don't tell anyone on the School Board I said so. I don't like it anymore than you do, but we have to face the reality of hiring practices in Hawaii."

The impact of Dr. Curtis's words had sent my heart racing.

"Maybe my mother is right," I allowed myself to reconsider. "Felice and I will never find a teaching job on Oahu." I pushed such a conclusion out of my mind. I refused to believe such a depressing thought.

"Once the School District realises what dynamic teachers we are, they'll relent," I told myself. "Mother can't be right."

Teri'i had saved us again. He created a way to make the practicum placements work. He had noticed my tears when I had finally got to the hotel the day that the practicum placements had been announced and he asked me what was wrong.

"Felice and I have been placed all the way out in Waianae and Wahiawa for our teaching practicum. I guess we'll have to quit our jobs with the Tropical Palace. We won't have enough time to get all the way to the Leeward Coast on the bus in the morning or get back for the band practices in the afternoon. I don't know how we are going to manage the school fees. Perhaps the bank will give us a loan."

"Teri'i solve problem," he beamed. "Teri'i let Kimi drive car fo her try teach Teri'i reading all dis time. She borrow car in morning. Drop Felice Wahiawa. Den Kimi and Felice pick Teri'i up on way to Tropical Palace later."

"You would let me take your car? All the way to Waianae?" I knew it was his prize possession.

"Sure, Teri'i do anyting fo Kimi."

"I'll never be able to repay you," I gasped.

"Teri'i find way, Kimi, promise."

So far he hadn't and Felice and I were half-way through our placements already. We owed Teri'i so much. But I wasn't having as much luck teaching him to read. I didn't understand it. He was obviously smart. You only had to tell him something once and he remembered it forever. But reading. He seemed to read from right to left instead of left to right. It took weeks for him to get to recognize even simple words and then one morning they seemed to go completely out of his head.

I'd asked Dr. Curtis about the problem and he said that he had seen students like Teri'i before. They were obviously intelligent but somehow they just couldn't develop reading above a beginning level.

"Just be glad your young friend has musical talent, Miss Kai`ika. He's going to have to find some young woman to do his reading for him, I'm afraid."

I hadn't had the heart to pass that advice on to Teri'i. He wanted to read so hard it nearly broke my heart.

"Kimi, what's all that stuff piled in front of Teri'i's door?" Felice asked as we carried over her baking. Clothes, musical instruments of all kinds, sheet music and books were all over the hallway.

I looked at the sheet music. It was all music for ukeleles and guitars.

"Kimi, Felice, come in," Teri'i called as he noticed us staring at the collection of belongings at his open door.

"No worry," he said at our startled expressions.

"Just Ito Nimura's stuff."

"Our Ito Nimura, the ukelele player?" I said in astonishment. Ito lived with his wealthy retailer father in one of the better sections of Honolulu.

"Yes, Ito. His fadder kick out of house. Teri'i pay back Ito now. He found place fo Teri'i live wen come Oahu fo audition."

"This tenement is becoming a place for family rejects," Felice said sadly. "What happened to Ito?"

"Oh, don't feel bad, Felice-San." It was Ito under another pile of his belongings.

"I got an 'F' in Accounting at the University and my father found out. He accused me of shaming the family."

"You're still taking Accounting at the University, Ito?" I was astonished. I thought all Ito was interested in was playing instruments. I'd never seen him do anything else but play ukelele and steel guitar. Even on his own time he was always jamming with other musicians at the hotel."

"I thought you dropped that course," I added.

"I should have. Instead, I ignored it. I don't think I made it to more than seven classes this past semester. I didn't think anyone would miss me but the instructor was keeping attendance. I knew I could pass by just studying the textbook but the instructor is one of those stickler types. Even thought I got an 'A' on all the exams in the course, he's failed me for poor attendance."

"That's terrible," Felice sympathized.

"Father-san gave me a choice when he looked at my mark. He said I had to quit my job at the hotel and pay more attention to my studies or he wouldn't pay my University fees. We got into a big argument and he kicked me out of the house until I come to my senses."

"Can't you pay for your own school fees?" I queried. "Like Felice and I do?"

"Ito-San doesn't want to be an accountant, Kimi. He wants to be the world's greatest ukelele player."

"But Ito, you're walking away from a University degree?" I started to argue with him. "And musicians in Hawaii hardly make enought to survive. Shouldn't you think this over?" I tried to reason with the short but likeable guy. He had all the entertainers in stitches up at the Tropical Palace with the comic hulas he kept putting together. Winston Emory was nuts about his latests hula. He had us all practicing it for the pilot film some guy was making for tourist promotion.

"Beautiful Kimi," Ito laughed. "Don't worry about Ito-san. Besides, you sound like Father-san."

"Felice, you bake?" Ito stared at her holeless donuts with considerable interest.

"Listen guys," he said. "It's Sunday. There's no show today. How about Ito-san go down to his favorite Deli for some Suishi and we all go on a picnic. I know a terrific surfing place. We'll take my ukelele and my surf board and have a great time."

"You have surf board, Ito?"

"Sure Teri'i-san. And baseball, golf, soccer equipment, even a complete croquet set. Our family chauffeur just dropped it all off on your sidewalk. Maybe we can set up the croquet set in the back yard."

"My family always bought me everything," he explained at our expressions.

"But who wants to be an accountant? You ever see a happy accountant, Teri'i-san? No way am I going to stop playing music. It's the love of my life."

"Ito, other than you, I've never heard of a Japanese ukelele player," I commented. I still wanted Ito to consider finishing his degree.

"Tell me how come you're so different from all the other Japanese Hawaiians. They all seem quite content becoming professionals of some kind or another. Our Normal School program has many Japanese students. Dr. Curtis says that Haoles, Chinese and Japanese students will be the only ones who can afford a four year program when it switches to the University of Hawaii next year."

"I don't know why Ito-san is so different," Ito sighed. I caught a hint of tears under his joking demeanor. I realised Ito was more upset about being kicked out of his home than he was letting on.

"To be truthful I never really fit in my family. They go to a Shinto shrine, I study Zen. They worship classical music. I like Hawaiian slack key and steel guitar. They live around Diamond Head in a huge house with servants. They want me to marry a Japanese high-mucky-muck, picture bride, and be an accountant in my father's business. I want to marry a beautiful hula maiden like Felice and be an entertainer. Ukelele music and comic hulas are forever flowing into my mind."

Ito scratched his head in wonderment and then broke into his customary beam.

"But now I live in Kalihi with Teri'i, Kimi and Felice," Ito joked. "Japanese always surrounded by family. Now Teri'i-san, Felice-san, and Kimi-san, even if she sound like Father-san, can be Ito's new family. Maybe it's all for the best. Let's to to the beach," he concluded.

"I wish I could have your attitude, Ito," Felice said sadly. "I still miss my family something awful."

"Ito," I tried again. "What are you doing moving in with Teri'i in this old house. How are you going to concentrate on your music with all the noise that goes on in this tenement. And aren't you used to more luxurious surroundings? You're never going to be comfortable here. Go speak to your father again. I'm sure he'll reconsider if you promise to study harder. Or at the very least find a suite for yourself. Somewhere you can be alone."

"You don't understand how we Japanese think, Kimi-san," Ito said in an unusually serious tone for him. "We don't like to be alone. Japanese families are very big. More than one generation in a house. Everything belongs to the whole family. We don't value individual achievement like Americans do. We value the whole family achieving together. I'd go nuts if I had to live all by myself. All my life I've had sisters, brothers, aunts, uncles, parents, grandparents all around me."

"Now, you, Felice-san, and Teri'i-san can be Ito's new family. We can all live and work together, grow wealthy together. As entertainers. Emory-san tells me that my comic hulas are going to be a big hit on the mainland, not just in Hawaii. We'll all share in the success."

"Ito, what's wrong with your own family?" I was beginning to think he'd lost his mind or something. "Why can't you be successful with them?"

"I can't be an accountant. I need to live with entertainers, not business people. I know it in my heart. It's hopeless." Ito's eyes filled with tears.

"Father-san will never accept a ukelele player in his family," he choked. "Ito-san will never be able to be an accountant. He has to form a new family. A family of entertainers."

"Ito, Felice and I can't be your family," I tried to make him see reality. "Felice and I are going to be teachers, not entertainers for life."

"Have mo understanding, Kimi," Teri'i interrupted me. I could tell he was really feeling Ito's pain.

"Teri'i, Felice, Kimi, come wit you on picnic, Ito," he promised.

"Too much work lately. All we do. We need party. I go Deli, Ito. You finish unpacking. Maybe get Kimi surf. She need play."

"Teri'i," I protested. "Felice and I have lesson plans to finish for morning."

"I'm going surfing, Kimi," Felice agreed with Teri'i. "We can do the lesson plans when we get back. Come on, the least you can do is help cheer Ito up. After all, we haven't had any fun since we started Normal School. And that's getting close to two years now."

It was emotional blackmail. Against my better judgement I agreed to go picnicking. That's when the disaster happened.

It was after we had eaten our picnic lunch. Teri'i came in from surfing and Ito had taken Felice to surf some waves quite a way offshore. I was leaning on a log sunning myself. I was determined to get some of my lesson plans out of the way and I was half-way through them. Teri'i stared at my back in horror.

"Kimi," he warned. "Back look like lobster, Teri'i put sun burn lotion on back."

"Don't be ridiculous," I argued. "I've only been in the sun for half-an-hour."

"Kimi lost time," Teri'i informed me. I glanced at my watch in alarm. "He's right," I thought. Somehow I had lost two hours.

"That always happens when I concentrate," I sighed.

Teri'i applied the lotion lightly to my back. "That's enough," I complained as he seemed to want to go on forever spreading lotion on my back.

"Kimi let Teri'i kiss her?" he asked suddenly, giving me full eye contact and looking very plaintive. I should have immediately said "No" but I was feeling very grateful for all the nurturing things that Teri'i kept doing for Felice and I.

"What harm can a kiss do?" I allowed myself to think. Teri'i moved closer and gently pulled me against him. I had never been so close to him before. He pressed his lips against mine. I relaxed and his tongue pressed tenderly into my mouth. We kissed slowly and then suddenly our bodies seemed to fit together as if they were made to.

Excitement flooded my body. I'd never felt so much attraction to anyone before. I could faintly hear some part of my mind telling me to break off contact. That becoming a teacher was the only important thing in my life.

"How am I supposed to resist him?" another side of my mind

seemed to be arguing back. "He's gorgeous." Teri'i was the one who finally released himself after what seemed an eternity.

"Kimi good kisser," he said. I felt my face grow beet red.

"Kimi date Teri'i?" he said cautiously. Instantly my mind was thrown into some kind of turmoil.

"Say no, Kimi," one part of my mind told me. "You have to concentrate on teaching."

"Say yes, Kimi," another side told me. "You know there's other women chasing Teri'i."

"Say no, Kimi," the argument continued in my mind. "You know Teri'i will never be anything but an entertainer."

"Say yes, Kimi," the other side shot back. "He's gorgeous, kind, loyal, and has all the characteristics you would want in a boyfriend."

Then Teri'i kissed me again, this time without asking. I lost all sense of where I was.

"Yes, Teri'i," I gasped several minutes later. "Kimi date Teri'i." He burst into a great big smile.

"Kimi no be sorry," he promised.

The next thing I knew we became a foursome. Felice was dating Ito Nimura. Once I started dating Teri'i, Ito and felice came everywhere with us. I guess that's what led to their engagement. They surprised us one afternoon just before show time.

"Kimi," Felice yelled. She flashed her left hand in front of my face. I glanced closely and noticed the huge diamond ring she was wearing on her left hand.

"That's beautiful but what does it mean?"

"Ito asked me to marry him. Not yet but in a year or two when we can both put a down payment on a home. " Band practice interrupted our conversation. All the entertainers congratulated Ito and Felice. I questioned her closely as soon as we reached our rented room.

"Felice," I protested. "You hardly know Ito. At least we've lived close to Teri'i for over a year. We see him everyday driving him to the Tropical Palace. But you've only become really closely acquainted with Ito for a month."

"I feel like I've known Ito all my life. And when he kisses me it feels like the ground is moving."

I grew silent as I realised Felice was as infatuated with Ito as I was with Teri'i.

"How is all this going to end up?" I asked feeling out of control at the sudden events.

"What are you going to do when we get our teacher certificates. That's only a few months away now."

"Why, just go on the same. Don't worry. You won't have to find a new roommate until Ito and I actually get married."

My mind reeled. I wondered how Felice could allow herself to marry an entertainer.

"I just know she's going to have to make a choice between being a teacher and running off somewhere with Ito so he can pursue his obsession with being a ukelele player." One side of my mind told me that I was going to have to decide what to do with Teri'i, too. Sometimes when Teri'i was so sweet like when he cooked dinner and romanced me on the weekend, Another side of my brain told me I was a dupe for falling for someone so different from me.

"What if Ito wants to leave Hawaii, Felice? You know he's determined to be the world's greatest ukelele player."

"Who knows! But at least I have someone in the world who cares about me now."

"We've got to go to that Family Planning Clinic. In case things get even more serious."

"You're impossible. You always want to plan everything years in advance. Can't you just let nature take it's course. Besides, I'm a Catholic. Catholics aren't supposed to practice birth control. I can't be seen going into that place."

"Face it, you were a Catholic. Father Julius took care of that for you. Besides, if you're really interested in Ito maybe you had better study Zen."

"You're impossible,"

I told Tutu about Felice becoming engaged and my feelings about Teri'i the next time I met her at the Laundry.

"Good someting nice finally happen fo Felice."

"Don't you think she should have waited till she found a teacher or someone professional, Tutu?"

"Mo important follow heart. She lucky Ito is nice man. And earn good leeving as ukelele player."

"I think I'm falling in love with Teri'i," I brought myself to confess my confusion. "But I don't know how he's going to fit into my life. What if I have to go to some remote place to teach. Teri'i's not going to want to go back to working on a plantation and plantation jobs are all that's available in the country."

"Follow heart, Kimi, like Felice. Hawaiians need follow Aloha witin. It work out somehow, you see."

"You always understand everything, Tutu."

"I no tell Mother. She not like you dating Tahitian fire dancer or Felice marry comic hula composer. Bad enough you dance fake hula."

"Oh, for Heaven's sake. Why can't Mother realise that time moves on. That we live in another era."

"You, Mother, mo like each udder den know Kimi. Both stubborn. Some day one of you must geev. Tutu wait. Best day of life wen Kimi, Mother reach understanding."

"Don't hold your breath," I said bitterly. "All my life, until recently, I was the one that had to give in. It's Mother's turn now."

Chapter 14.

Guatemala.

The yacht trip to Guatemala was the most exciting event in my life since I met Atherton on a luxury liner cruising from London to New York. Norman had taken care of every possible detail for me. He had even been thoughtful enough to bring a friend of mine, Julia Bridgewater, along as a chaperone. Julia and I had become good friends since I had joined her in her endeavors to stop billboards from spoiling the beauty of Diamond Head. Atherton had agreed at once to my going to Guatemala with Norman once he understood that Julia would be going with me.

"Jessica," Julia questioned me one day as we lazed, sipping cocktails in comfortable deck chairs staring at the whitecaps on the ocean. "Why is Norman Baker going to all this trouble for you?"

"What do you mean? Why, Norman is just repaying me for being the official dinner and special-event hostess for his company for the last two years."

"Sure Jessica! And he doesn't have some other motive for this trip? Do you realise this is the first time Norman has taken a holiday since his wife, Dorothy's death three years ago."

"Norman mentioned something about investments in Guatemala," I confessed. "But I swear I don't have the slightest idea what he's thinking of. And I couldn't possible invest, anyway.

All my money is tied up in Atherton's latest venture with the Tropical Palace Hotel."

"Have you noticed how Norman looks at you? I swear there's more on his mind than just rewarding you for your hostess endeavours."

"Oh, don't be silly. Why, it's just that Norman and I have a lot in common. He likely thinks of me as the daughter he never had. And I must confess I lose all track of time when I'm with Norman."

"Norman isn't looking at you in a fatherly way, believe me. Why the temperature in the room heats up noticeably when both of you are together. You mean to tell me all those nights you've acted as Norman's hostess, he's never made advances towards you. Why, half of Honolulu thinks you and Norman are having an affair."

"To tell you the truth," I confessed, "I would have found an offer of an affair with Norman very tempting. After all, he is everything Atherton is not. But Norman's always been a perfect gentleman in my presence."

"If you say so," Julia's voice expressed disbelief. "And I suppose it wasn't my husband that told you about the Tropical Palace being up for sale, either? Michael was so mad when Atherton snatched that interest up before he could purchase it himself. How did you hear about the deal, anyway, and how come you put up the money up for another of Atherton's ventures? Michael told me the Tropical Palace deal was being kept a secret, and the last time Atherton's investment went sour I remember you saying you wouldn't back him again."

I realised that Julia was doing a little discrete prying into how well I knew her husband.

"Oh, Theodore Wiltshire told Atherton about this deal. And I couldn't stand Atherton's whining until I invested." There was no way Julia was going to get me to confess that Michael Bridgewater, himself, had recommended investing in the Tropical Palace hotel.

I was saved from further prying by our arrival to Guatemala.

We had arrived in San Jose Harbor. We had to anchor as the harbor was too shallow for the huge yacht. A strange bucket and rope contraption transported our luggage and then us to the dock. Norman took both of us to a waiting limousine.

"Don't worry about clearing Customs," he informed us. "I've already taken care of everything."

The driver escorted all three of us to the back of the limousine and then moved into the front of the vehicle himself. I couldn't believe the high standard of living the upper class in Guatemala enjoyed as we drove the seven mile journey into Guatemala City.

In one section of the city, palatial mansions stood next to each other enclosed by well-kept and landscaped acreages. The car stopped at a particularly luxurious estate and the driver got out to open the gate. I stared at the red tiled roof and white plaster outside of the mansion.

"I've rented this private estate for our stay in Guatemala," Norman told Julia and I. I realised that he had taken care of every detail in his usual fashion.

The next day I was having lunch with Julia while we were waiting for Norman to return from a business conference.

"I was expecting some hardships on this trip," I said to Julia. "Going to a foreign country and all. Perhaps food that couldn't be eaten or locals begging for money. I thought we would have to take care of our own hair ourselves, too. But so far we've been taken care of better than when we're at home in Honolulu."

"I know," she laughed. "Both of our husbands could learn from Norman Baker about how to properly care for women of our class. And can you believe that the servants here actually seem even eager to please you. Why back in Honolulu servants seem to have an air that they're doing you a tremendous favor by being employed by you," Julia mused.

"Jessica, the limousine is ready for our trip to the coffee plantation. Julia, My Dear, I've arranged another limousine and a trusted colleague to show you some of the sights of the city."

It was Norman arriving with some exceedingly handsome South American man.

"This is Manuel Cruz, ladies," he's my Vice-president, here, for my operations in Guatemala." Julia stared at Manuel's exotice good looks with open admiration.

"Julia, I've asked Manuel to show you around the city. I didn't want to bore you with the coffee plantation that I want Jessica to invest in."

"How kind of you." Julia went willingly off in the company of Manuel Cruz.

"Maybe now she won't be too nosy about my private life," I found myself thinking.

I turned and looked at Norman with approval. He was dressed rather casually for him in a sports jacket and matching slacks. It made him lose ten years.

"You look years younger without the formal business suits you wear at the office," I commented.

"In that case, My Dear, I'll dress in nothing else but sport jackets and casual slacks forever, I promise."

We made our way out of the lavish estate house that Norman had rented for our stay and into a polished, black limousine. The chauffeur closed the back door with proper deference and moved behind the wheel. The car was so well constructed that ruts in the road could hardly be felt.

"If Atherton was arranging this trip," I complained, "we'd probably be driving in some bouncing sport car. He seems addicted to the things. This is a much more civilized way to travel."

"You deserve the best," Norman said softly, lightly touching my hand. My heart warmed. For the past three weeks Norman had taken care of every detail to keep Julia and I comfortable and pleased. I couldn't believe that the cooks on the yacht and the estate had been briefed in advance on our culinary likes and dislikes. Even our favorite hairdressers had been transplanted from Honolulu to arrange our hair every morning.

I glanced out the window at the passing agricultural fields.

They were mostly bananas, sugarcane and cotton. As we came to what looked like a fairly new agricultural area coffee and sugarcane seemed to be thriving as well as they did on the Big Island and Oahu.

"When did coffee and sugar start being planted here? They look like they've been planted fairly recently."

"That observation is very astute of you, My Dear. Coffee has been growing in this area for years but the sugarcane is a recent experiment. I've had the woods deforested and squatters removed to plant these crops. You see I'm becoming increasingly concerned about the growing union organizational threat in Hawaii. Why, we had to resort to opening fire in Hilo to stop picketing. And that Filipino agitator on the plantations; we had to see that he was run out of the county for good."

"What you are viewing here is my diversification plan." Norman told me that it was that sugar and pineapple would become too costly to grow in Hawaii sometime in the future because of union agitation for better wages. He added that it was also possible that the land that was now under cultivation in Hawaii would be worth more for resort and housing development some day. He told me that to take care of those possibilities he had transferred some of his assets out of the country and that he was preparing to vastly extend his lands in coffee, sugarcane and cotton under cultivation here in Guatemala.

"You mean that sugar and coffee can be grown here cheaper that Hawaii?"

"It's pretty equivalent, now, My Dear, even with greater transportation costs." Norman told me that Guatemala was similar to what Hawaii was fifty years ago with a cheap labor supply, good land with agricultural possibilites that could be bought or leased for very little from the government, providing the right political pockets were greased, and that there was no sign of the labor force revolting or banding together. He said that Guatemala had just the conditions necessary to maximize profits and that the government knew how to deal with dissidents. Norman said that if the plantation workers didn't smarten up in Hawaii, he would just transfer more of his business interests to Guatemala.

"How clever of you. That's something that Atherton wouldn't even think of, I know. He does nothing but complain about the rising wages the Tropical Palace is forced to pay it's chambermaids and food handlers but never thinks about a contingency plan."

"I want you to consider investing in this agricultural acreage with me, Jessica."

I started. What Norman was proposing was a complete shock.

"Why I would love to, but my assets are tied up in the Tropical Palace hotel right now."

Norman put his arm around my shoulders as if to steady me. I braced myself for what he was going to say. He looked very serious.

"Jessica, I'm going to offer Atherton a deal. I'll buy out your investment in the Tropical Palace, and transfer it and my interest in the hotel into Atherton's name if he'll agree to a divorce from you. That should give Atherton a controlling interest in the hotel. Then I'll invest the equivalent amount in your name in the coffee, cotton, sugar-cane and agricultural acreage here, provided you agree to become my wife."

"Norman, marriage? And you're talking millions," I gasped.

"A drop in the bucket of my assets. As you know I don't have an heir and I'm not prepared to leave my money to those nitwit sons my brother spawned. You give me hope that I might have an heir yet."

I couldn't believe Norman's proposition. I was shaking violently as I thought of the implications of his proposal.

"I would be free of Atherton, a husband I could no longer admire, my marriage to Norman would make me the leading lady of Honolulu society, and my children would inherit a fortune," I reasoned. "And on top of that I would be married to a real man."

"Unless, of course, you consider a marriage with me the last thing you would be interested in, My Dear. Believe me, I'll understand if you think our age difference is too great to overcome."

"Norman, I find you devilishly attractive," I confessed. "And besides, you look and act years younger than Atherton."

Norman's features went into a vastly relieved look.

"Take time to consider this," he ordered.

The limousine had drawn up to one of the fields. I needed the hand that the chauffeur had extended as I tried to move out of the car. I was still shaking from Norman's proposition. I couldn't believe what a wonderful man he was. All this time I'd been expecting a discreet flirtation and he had been working on a way to make our relationship permanent. I couldn't believe such an opportunity to change my circumstances in life had come along. And I would be married to a man who knew how to turn everything he invested into gold.

"Maybe I might be able to provide Norman with a son of his own," I thought, excitement flooding my being. "After all I haven't reached the end of my child bearing years yet."

Back at the estate house, hours later, I couldn't remember anything about the layout of the coffee plantation.

"Norman's words must have sent me reeling," I realised.

"Norman, what have you done with Julia Bridgewater?" I queried. "There was still no sign of either her or Manuel Cruz." Norman laughed.

"Just let's say that I'm having her entertained in a style she wouldn't be able to refuse. I wanted some time alone with you."

"Norman, Dear, are you sure you would welcome the thought of a child?" I queried as he poured me for a sherry.

"Any man my age would be overjoyed to be presented with a child. Does that mean you accept my proposition?"

"Yes, Dear." Norman pulled me against his body tightly and kissed me. I couldn't believe the strength of my response. After several minutes Norman broke off our embrace.

"We'll wait until my lawyers reach a successful negotiation with Atherton, Jessica," he ordered.

"We must be discreet, I don't want viscious gossip to detract from the joy of our years together."

I took a deep breath and managed to keep my desires in bounds. I couldn't believe Norman's strength of mind. "He's everything Atherton is not," I thought again. "My luck must have changed forever."

Just then Julia and Manuel Cruz came charging into the living room. Manuel looked apologetically at Norman.

I breathed a sigh of relief as Norman had released his grasp on me and we were sitting quite apart.

"Jessica," Julia ordered. "I insist you and Norman join Manuel and I for a night out on the town. You have no idea what exciting dining and dancing places Manuel has showed me. And the marimbas. You have no idea how many ways there are to play a marimba. Come on, it will do the both of you good to live a little for a change."

"Why, we would be delighted, wouldn't we Jessica?"

"Indeed," I replied. "I wonder if there's anywhere where they are doing the tango? I must confess that the first time I danced the tango was on that cruise from New York to London when I met Atherton."

"The tango is danced everywhere," Julia testified. "And you have no idea how many different ways there are to dance it. Manuel has showed me every one, I swear."

Chapter 15.

Disillusionment.

It was months after the graduation ceremony from the Territorial Normal School that Felice and I were forced to acknowledge we would never have even temporary teaching positions in an urban area on Oahu. It was already the end of August and we hadn't even reached the short-list for any of the urban area openings. Even in rural areas closer to Honolulu we weren't given serious consideration.

"It's like my mother told me, Felice," I sobbed. "I never believed her but she's right. Only Haoles are allowed to be teachers in Honolulu."

"What are we going to do? You know Mr. Emory is taking the hotel band to California. And Ito and Teri'i as well as us have been invited to go with him. Mr. Scully has managed to find a replacement band for the Tropical Palace."

"I don't know what to do," I confessed, tears streaming down my face. "I can't bear to go through any more of those fake interviews where the Principal of the school pretends to be impressed by my excellent scholastic record and recommendations then never hires me."

"Perhaps we could use you as a substitute, Miss Kai`ika," they all tell me. "Ordinarily we don't hire natives in this area but if our parents approve of you I suppose we could make an exception."

"I know what you mean. You should have felt the atmosphere in that last Catholic school I was interviewed in. They called Father Julius because they'd asked me where I'd last attended Church services. He must have given them an earful. I've never been ushered out of a job interview so fast. I didn't even get a letter of rejection from them."

"There must be something we can do." I desperately searched my mind for a ray of hope of some kind.

"Dr. Curtis says we just have to keep trying, Felice. He's convinced we'll eventually get jobs on Molokai or Kauai if openings come up."

"Do you know how lonely Molokai or Kauai would be without Ito or Teri'i?"

"Maybe they'd come with us." I was convinced Teri'i would do anything for me.

"Not Ito. He loves his ukelele more than he loves me, I know it. Besides, we'd have to be married for the School Board to tolerate us living with someone. And even if Ito and Teri'i married us, and I know Teri'i doesn't want to get married for a while yet, School Superintendents don't want to hire young, married teachers. They know they're sure to have children before long and they'll have to be replaced."

"Don't panic. They'll put us on the substitute list, if nothing else. If Teri'i's still willing to drive us all over the Island we can support ourselves for awhile from substituting for regular teachers."

"Kimi, Mr. Scully has hired another band and group of entertainers until Winston Emory can return to Waikiki. Ito and Teri'i will be unemployed if they remain here."

"And, do you realise what you're asking me to turn down. Five times the salary of a regular teacher, a trip to the mainland, a chance to become a star and Ito's company. Just to substitute occasionally in some school. You're crazy, if you ask me."

"But entertainment isn't for forever. How long do you think Hawaiian music will be a craze on the mainland?"

"By that time maybe Ito and I will have saved enough money for a house here on Oahu. You and Teri'i could do the same. After all you and I can always go back to teaching at a later date. Maybe they'll be willing to let Hawaiian teachers teach Haole students by that time."

To my shock, even Teri'i wasn't as sympathetic as he'd always been before.

"Kimi, teaching losing proposition. Waste time. Tell you befo. Pay nutting, teacher be old maid. Come California wit Teri'i and Ito-san. See America. Party. Be happy. Kimi leev good life with Teri'i."

"But," I argued, "all my life I've wanted to be a teacher. Won't you come to Kauai or the Big Island with me?"

"No Kimi." I felt like a knife had been placed in my heart. "Kimi very sweet but Kauai, Hilo mean Teri'i work plantation. No future."

"Maybe I could find a job in Kona. They use entertainers in some of the hotels there. Maybe you could get work in Kona."

"Kimi dream. Only plantation work deah. Kimi have teach in Plantation school, not Kona. Haole students, Kona, too. Same all ovah, Kimi. Only Haoles get be professionals."

"What do you mean?" I sobbed.

"Plantation Teri'i work Kauai. Only one engineer non-Hawaiian. He tird generation Chinese. Fadder put trough school. But Plantation no promote. Stay same job. Bring young, Haole engineer from mainland be boss engineer instead. Chinese engineer have train new, younger, Haole boss. He quit. Move to mainland."

I started to panic completely. Teri'i was sounding like my mother.

"Surely mother and Teri'i can't be right," I thought. But in my heart I knew by this time they were. Even Dr. Curtis had said that Felice and I would have to work in Hilo or Lihue and gradually work up to rural areas on Oahu if openings occurred.

"Kimi decide," Teri'i ordered. "Stay here, teach udder islands, be old maid or come California wit Teri'i, Felice and Ito." He left and my head went into a spin.

It was all too much for me. I realised I'd be lost without Teri'i. And I was going to be all alone. teaching in some rural area without hope of promotion or movement to an urban center on Oahu for years, maybe decades.

"I finally get what I worked for all these years, a teaching certificate, and it costs me my family, my best friend, and Teri'i," I broke down in tears. I couldn't decide what to do.

That afternoon I went to the laundry to speak to Tutu. The other employees kind of giggled to each other under their breaths as I came in. I guess they were expecting another shouting match like the one I'd had with my mother.

"Tutu, something terrible has happened," I whispered.

"I take break, Kimi," she said loudly.

We went out to the street and sat down under one of the palm trees that were swaying in the brisk trade wind that day. One without coconuts on it.

"How you know beeg pilikia, Kimi?" Tutu demanded.

"What pilikia?"

"Mudder go Big Island. Hilo. End month. She finally save money fo down payment old farm. Want grow orchids. She want Tutu go wit her and Kimo."

"Oh, no," I went into shock. "Now even Tutu's not going to be on Oahu anymore. I'm going to be completely alone,"

"You come Big Island, too, Kimi? Maybe get teacher job, Hilo."

"But what about Teri'i? He's going to California with Mr. Emory and the orchestra. He wants me to come with him."

"Mother be furious. She tink you turn back on culture. Sell out to Haoles. She no want you do Tahitian Tamure in America wit fake fire dancer."

"Oh, for Pete's sake, This is 1937. Can't mother realize it's not ancient times anymore."

"Mother no listen. Mo bettah Kimi go Big Island. Teach deah.

Go back Hula Kahiko. Halau dance dere like old days. Mother be pleased."

I burst into tears.

"But Tutu," I sobbed. "I love Teri'i," I confessed. I couldn't believe the strength of my emotions. "How am I going to get along without him?"

Tutu smiled.

"Tutu test Kimi. Tutu tink you love Teri'i mo den you know." She nodded sagely.

"But what am I going to do?"

"Listen heart, Kimi. Listen Aloha witin. Hawaiian only true to self wen listen Aloha witin."

"America is so far away. What if I don't like it there?"

"Den Kimi come home. Tutu, Mother, Kimo be waiting on Big Island."

"Tutu, you understand so much," I cried. She gave me a big hug.

Chapter 16.

Changes.

The handgun was sitting in the right hand drawer of my desk. I seriously contemplated using it. Norman Baker's lawyers had finally left me to sort out my emotions.

"Give us a call by noon tomorrow at the latest, Scully," the tallest of the pair had ordered. "That offer's not going to be on the table forever," he warned. "Remember, you can be broke as well as wifeless if you want. It's your choice."

I couldn't breathe. My chest cavity felt like it had collapsed into itself. My head reeled. I finally allowed the tears that Baker's lawyers had caused to escape down my face. I put my head into my arms and sobbed brokenheartedly for what must have been an eternity. Hurt finally turned to anger and I pounded my desk savagely with the fist of my right hand over and over again.

"I'll never let Jessica go," I vowed. "Even if I wind up in the poor house, I'll never agree to a divorce."

"What's wrong, Mr. Scully?"

I started as I realised my young secretary was touching me gently on my back.

"Is there something I can do?" I could see concern written all over Noriko's face. I tried to grasp onto some vestige of control.

"It's my wife, Noriko," I found myself confessing. "She's asking me for a divorce? I had no idea that she must have been having an affair with that bastard, Norman Baker."

"A fine man like you," Noriko said soothingly. "Why Mrs. Scully must be out of her mind. You do nothing but try to please her."

"Never mind." I tried desperately to return to some semblance of rational thought.

"Please leave me alone and shut the door. Go home and take the rest of the day off. Keep this to yourself, of course. I need time to think. I reached towards the right hand drawer.

"I'm not leaving you at a time like this, Mr. Scully," Noriko sounded quietly determined.

"I know how much your wife meant to you. You were always sending me on errands to buy her presents, flowers and chocolates."

Noriko's words set me into sobbing again.

"I'll kill myself," I threatened. "Isn't that what you Japanese do when you are humiliated? It's the only way to get even with Jessica."

"Mr. Scully, think of your sons," Noriko advised. In Japanese family suicide over business failure is expected, but suicide over love causes great loss of face. Only business failure justifies suicide."

My secretary seemed genuinely alarmed.

"And remember the employees of this hotel. We depend on you for our livelihood. Don't cause a scandal that would destroy your sons and the Tropical Palace Hotel."

"Leaving me for a man old enough to be her father," I expressed some of the self-pity I felt.

"I'll be the laughingstock of Honolulu again."

"Mr. Scully, a man as clever, wealthy and handsome as you can find another woman." I gasped as Noriko me advised knowingly.

"Perhaps someone half your age and very beautiful. Surely that would be a more appropriate revenge on your wife than killing yourself."

Despite the state of my mind, I found myself giving a short laugh. Noriko's idea appealed to me.

"Noriko, I never realised you had such a diabolical side." I looked at my secretary with new interest. She was a very beautiful, unmarried, young woman. Her words seemed to have somehow taken the edge off of the pain in my heart.

"I moved you from Reception because you were so sweet and polite to everyone. I never imagined you'd be willing to even hurt so much as a fly."

"I do not wish to hurt anyone, Mr. Scully. But from the depth of your pain I can tell you think Mrs. Scully will not change her mind. She has chosen another. You should do the same."

"Thank you, Noriko," I tried to make my voice sound slightly amused. "For your advice. But I've been married to my wife for nearly thirty years. I would find it impossible to love another the way I've always loved Jessica. Now I insist you leave for the day and let me solve this problem in my own way."

I went into my private bathroom. Noriko was gone by the time I returned. I reached for the drawer in my desk the handgun was in. It was empty.

"What the Hell?" I cursed.

"Noriko," I shouted. I went into the next room. But Noriko had left as I'd ordered her.

"My God, she must have taken the gun," I realised. I went back into my office and stared out at the small balcony off my desk.

"Maybe if I threw myself off of that?" I thought. I slithered out onto the balcony and stared at the ground below.

"What if I don't die?" I thought. The drop was three stories but there was a garden at the bottom.

"What am I thinking of?" I realised as I went back into my office. "Killing myself is going to leave everything in Jessica's name. I'd only be doing her a favor."

I went down to the bar and sat heavily on one of the bar stools.

"A triple whisky and no chaser," I ordered.

I knocked down several of them before the pain in my heart seemed to be dulled slightly. I considered the offer Norman Baker's lawyer had presented.

"A controlling interest in the hotel in return for divorcing Jessica. Admitting to adultery I had never taken part in. It would all be arranged quite discreetly," they said.

"Talk about doubling your investment," I reasoned, my mind dulled by the alcohol. But Jessica's rejection of me made me feel absolutely humiliated. She hadn't even said one word to me about a divorce since returning from Guatemala.

"How could she have betrayed me this way, after all these years?"

"Of course, there was that affair with Michael Bridgewater. But someone old enough to be her father?"

"And all this time I thought she was doing me a favor being the old boy's hostess. I must have been spending too much time on hotel affairs not to have seen this coming." Then I thought of Noriko's advice.

"Maybe I could find some young woman half my age. What about Noriko, herself? She comes from a well respected family, even if it is Japanese," I realised.

The bartender refilled my glass. I gulped the liquor down. It hit me all of a sudden and I realised I was close to passing out. I knew there was something I had to do before I allowed myself to do that. I reached for the card Baker's lawyer had left in my pocket and signalled for the phone from the bar. I dialed the number.

"Draw up the papers," I ordered in a slurred voice.

"I knew you would see it Mr. Baker's way," the voice on the other end chortled. "We'll send a car right over." I managed to stagger to the hotel porch.

"It's the only thing I can do," I told myself as I waited for the lawyer's car. "This way I'll have a controlling interest in the Tropical Palace Hotel to leave my sons instead of a public scandal."

Chapter 17.

Journey To California.

"I wonder what it will be like to be back in the mainland again," I wondered to myself as I looked at Waikiki beach with mixed emotion. One part of myself was sad at leaving paradise and a race of people with so much Aloha. Not to mention an unending line of tourists that were highly appreciative of my adaptations to and redoing of Hawaiian music and culture. Another part of me was joyous at finally getting the recognition for my musical talent that I always knew I deserved back on the mainland.

My selfconfidence was soaring with the news that Hawaiian music was flying high on the recording charts all over the States thanks to both my adaptations and those of one of the other Hotel Music Directors in Waikiki.

"Boss Emory," my musing was cut short by one of my entertainers hailing me across the hotel's private beach area. "Teri'i, Ito, Kimi and Felice agree go California like you ask."

I smiled at Teri'i's enthusiasm.

"Good, Teri'i. I can use all the Polynesian entertainers I can get. But how did you get Kimi Kai`ika to agree to come with the band? I thought she was going to stay behind and try and find a teaching job on Oahu."

"Kimi have no luck wit job finding. Want Teri'i stay wit her. But say no. Force Kimi choose Teri'i or teaching job. Kimi choose

Teri'i." He beamed as only Teri'i could beam when he was extremely pleased.

"Good for you. Ito Nimura and Felice Santos have already given me their acceptance. Better say good-bye to Waikiki, we're going to have to leave at the end of the month."

"Not much time, Boss."

"I know, but my agent calls the shots. He wants all of us there by the start of the month."

"Big break fo you, Boss."

"Yes it is. Hawaiian music is the craze on the mainland. It's just like before the depression. Big bands everywhere. Thank Heavens the Hawaii gig came up for me just when it was looking like I might be a penniless bandleader for ever."

"Americans fond Hawaiian music?" I nodded just as Kimi Kai`ika came up to us and joined Teri'i."

"I understand you're coming with the band, Kimi?"

"Yes, Mr. Emory. But you are returning to Hawaii in a year, aren't you? I do have hopes of returning to teaching."

"One never really knows in show business. We're supposed to come back in a year but you never know what might come up for us. Maybe even a movie or bookings I can't refuse in New York or Las Vegas." I ignored Kimi's look of disappointment. I wasn't sure she had the right attitude to make it big in show business. I knew from my own experience that an entertainer had to sacrifice everything else for success.

"Take at look at this cover for this new sheet music by the Music Director of the other hotel, will you?" I asked the two entertainers I had with me. "It's just arrived and I want to play it in Los Angeles." I showed Kimi and Teri'i the cover for my key rival's new composition.

"Princess Poo-poo`-ly Has Plenty Pa-pa-ya (and she Loves to Give it Away)" Kimi read. I expected her enthusiastic praise but became shocked at her comments.

"Mr. Emory," she protested. "That Hawaiian woman on the cover is half naked."

I glanced more closely at the cover.

"Well the princess does have naked breasts, Kimi," I admitted, "but this is a cartoon cover. After all, 'Princess Poo-poo'-ly Has Plenty Pa-pa`ya' is meant to be funny."

"Not look like cartoon breasts, Boss," Teri'i commented. "Look real. American men love."

I ignored Kimi's facial expression of displeasure.

"You've got the right ideas on how to please audiences, Teri'i. I'm sure you'll go far in show business."

"What matter, Kimi?" Teri'i asked her.

"Cartoon or not, Princess Poo-poo-`ly is standing half naked with breasts that defy gravity and holding out her papayas to passer bys," Kimi argued. "My mother hates this kind of thing. She says that covers like that one and words like Princes Poo-poo`ly are ridiculing native Hawaiian culture and demeaning Hawaiian women."

"Well, to some, this cover does suggest multiple meanings, Kimi," I admitted. "I didn't write it but maybe I could suggest covering up the breasts a little to my colleague. But let's face it. Every ethnic group has to put up with some jokes at their expense. Why, forbid jokes about others and you wouldn't have one stand-up-comic left in America."

Teri'i and Kimi went off. I made one last stroll around the Waikiki waterfront and then walked over to Atherton Scully's office. His secretary Noriko told me to go right in. I gave Noriko a warm smile. There were rumors running through the hotel that she was going to become Scully's next wife now that Jessica Scully had divorced him.

"Thanks for freeing us for that California tour, Mr. Scully."

"Call me Atherton, Winston," he replied.

"I'm delighted to see you having success on the mainland. Your success means more customers for tourism in Hawaii. And maybe even movie goers. The Music Director from the other hotel has landed a movie contract, they tell me. Maybe you will too. They tell me that for every thousand people who attend a movie with a Hawaii theme or a Hawaiian music score we can expect ten tourists at least."

"And that flight in that new clipper airplane to Honolulu cuts days off travel to Hawaii, I understand."

"That's righ. Why one of these days Hawaii is going to be accessed by even Americans of limited means."

"You'll have to build cheaper hotels, Atherton, if you want people of limited means to come here."

"That's not a bad idea. At least accomodations for middle-class Americans. I imagine some entrepreneur will cotton on to that idea."

"We'll expect you back in exactly one year, Winston. The other band has agreed to play for us until then."

"That's what I expect unless something unforeseen happens."

"Don't worry if that's the case. As I say the more your music that tells of the beauty of Hawaiian women, surf and sea succeeds in mainstream America the more tourists will be drawn here by the siren songs. Don't worry, we'll manage in your absence."

Despite the pressure to pack I couldn't resist another trip around the beach area. Kimi's criticism of the Princess Poo-poo'-ly cover stung, though.

"It's a good thing that young lady has a teaching certificate," I thought, "and that she's infatuated with Teri'i. She really doesn't have the right attitude for show business."

"It's going to be funny leaving here. Why, I only came here for six months and they turned into years. And it's all thanks to Auntie Edith Hoaloha. I was completely frozen trying to get ideas for that musical medley that Atherton Scully wanted for the charter Malolo passengers. Without Auntie's help I would never have gotten that medley together."

"I wonder if she's ever figured out that I wasn't one of Dr. Schweitzer's students like she thought. Too bad I had to fool her, but look what my adaptations to the music she showed me have done for Hawaiian tourism. I'm sure with that radio show that beams to the mainland, Hawaiian music must have lured thousands to Hawaii. Surely I can be forgiven for a little deception."

"California is going to be a shock for my Hawaiian entertainers, though, at least the ones with dark skins. I haven't told them yet but they are going to have to live with the color restrictions in California. That's going to be a big pain. My Caucasian entertainers are going to be able to stay in hotels near where the gigs are but any entertainers with darker skin are going to have to be located somewhere where colored people are put up. What a nightmare for organization."

Chapter 18.

On The Mainland.

I watched Felice scurry as she disappeared out of the lounge that Ito, Teri'i, and I were having lunch in.

"It's all so complicated for Felice on the mainland, Ito," I remarked with a sigh.

"Most of the time Felice passes for white and it's safe for her to use the white womans' washroom. But if she's been sitting in public with us she's likely to get arrested or at the very least thrown out of the lounge if she doesn't use the segregated washroom."

"These color issues pass understanding, Kimi-san," Ito replied. "I feel deeply for Felice. She doesn't seem to fit solidly in the American color hierarchy with her Hawaiian and Portuguese background and her white skin."

"At least in Hawaii color barriers are more subtle. The first time I realised the extent of the Haole color bars was when Felice and I were turned down time and again for teaching jobs in schools with Haole children." Ito sighed.

"The only way I can cope with such issues, Kimi-san, is to turn inward. Use Zen meditation exercises. There I get glimpses that reality is really composed of energy. It's so stupid to think that the amount of Melanin in one's skin somehow determines the pecking order you'll be in for life."

I was surprised at how serious Ito was. He usually just joked about serious issues.

"California must really be getting to him," I thought.

"God, Kimi, those washrooms aren't even clean," Felice complained as she rejoined us. "How can they have such different standards for people of color?"

"I told you guys to go befo we went out," Teri'i stated. "Dis not Hawaii anymore."

"But Teri'i," Felice groaned. "If only we'd gone to New York with some of the other Hawaiian entertainers instead of to California with Mr. Emory."

"Color bars are likely not that different in New York," I argued. I was having trouble myself adjusting to mainland America.

"Just be glad we didn't go on that jazz tour to the deep South." I could hear blame in Felice's voice.

"It's not my fault, Felice-san, that we wound up in California. Emory-san say he have to honor contract."

"Think of money, ladies," Teri'i added. "California gigs pay big bucks. Wat small discomfort in washroom? Plan ahead better."

"You right Teri'i-San," Ito went back to his usual jolly self. "Hawaiian music new craze in America. Openings all over. Maybe even Japan."

"Besides," Teri'i added, "Boss Emory say go New York soon. He promise. Also mo movies want fire dancers and comic hula. You see. We be rich. Other Hotel Music Director big star now. Score music for Hollywood. Soon pay off big fo Mr. Emory, too."

"I thought we were going back to Hawaii in six months or a year?" I queried.

"Tings change, Kimi. Boss Emory become beeg star heah. Say have take advantage of offers while dey hot. Teri'i, Kimi, Ito, Felice become wealthy quick, you see."

"Color bars exist even if you're wealthy," I protested. "We're still not going to be any better off in New York."

"No matter. Save money. Go back Hawaii, few years or maybe

Tahiti. Buy beeg house, good neighborhood. Forget what happen mainland."

"When Teri'i?" I argued. "Twenty years from now at the rate we're saving money."

"Teri'i need dat new car. Drive Kimi, Felice, Ito, to gigs. We no allowed stay most neighborhood where gigs are."

"I hate those segregated, rat traps. I'm not going to share my life with cockroaches for anything."

"Then no worry. We pay car quick. One year. Den save for house."

"If you say so." I stopped arguing but inwardly I felt sick. I'd never stopped regretting my decision to leave Hawaii. As much fun as it was to be with Ito and Teri'i, I'd never got used to the degree of the racism on the mainland. In Hawaii, maybe I couldn't teach in white neighborhoods but I was somebody. In California white women seemed to appreciate us on the stage all right, particularly Teri'i with his looks, but how they'd react with righteous anger if they found us in their washrooms or their color restricted apartment blocks.

"It had all happened so fast," I recalled. Felice and I had no sooner agreed to go to California with Ito and Teri'i, then Mr. Emory decided to go even sooner than we were supposed to. He promised to bring us to back to Hawaii as soon as he honored his commitments but they were dragging on longer than expected and he didn't like to turn down new contracts.

I was really hoping that when the first contract was finished Mr. Emory would go back to the Tropical Palace Hotel. That way Felice and I could at least go back to substitute teaching. To my horror, I was beginning to see my mother's point of view about fake Hawaiian music. In California, Hawaiian music was even more diluted by the addition of famous musicians that audiences came to see like the drummer Mr. Emory had hired. The drummer was great and audiences loved him but there was nothing Hawaiian about his playing. Even I had to acknowledge that our music really had little to do with authentic Hawaiian culture.

"Californians just came to escape the drudgery of their daytime jobs and escape into the romantic fantasies our revue offers them," I thought. "They dream of an escape to Hawaii one night and the next they go somewhere else and lose themselves in jazz."

"Too bad the California School Board told us our teaching certificates were not recognised here, Kimi."

I started as I realised Felice was thinking the same thoughts I was.

"I know. But when Winston Emory offered us that long-term contract if we came to California we couldn't refuse, I suppose. He offered us more money than we'd make in five years in Hawaii."

"Now you tinking better, Kimi!" Teri'i said.

Too bad about the California School Board, though," Ito at least understood our plight.

"Teaching certificates from Hawaii," they'd sneered. "Maybe in the Ozarks, but we're not prepared to accept your credentials here." They wouldn't even let us substitute.

"I wonder how much longer we will be in California?" Ito mused. He seemed to be growing more moodier the longer we stayed on the mainland. Felice had confided that Ito was worried about his brother attending university in Tokyo."

"Ito's worrying about the growing tension between Japan and the United States," Felice told me. "He's afraid his brother is going to get drafted into the Japanese army. Too bad his father thinks the University of Japan is far superior to the University of Hawaii. He made Kenji transfer."

"Felice, let's get married at the end of the month!"

I couldn't believe my ears. Ito was setting a wedding date in the middle of a crowded lounge in Los Angeles. Vitori's jaw dropped open a mile. Felice's eyes welled up with tears.

"Ito, you lose mind!" Teri'i gasped.

"No, Teri'i-san, time to marry Felice-san. Make sense. Ito-san love Felice. Felice-san love Ito-san? World getting scary.

Who knows what big countries do in future? At least Ito be with Felice."

"Yes, Ito. We'll get married at the end of the month." Felice appeared to have made up her mind. The two of them kissed each other in the lounge. Teri'i and I stared at each other in complete amazement.

"Maybe we make it a double ceremony, Teri'i-san?"

My heart pounded. Ito was confronting my fears of marrying Teri'i so soon.

"Ito, marriage isn't something you order for lunch in a lounge," I complained.

"End of month. We go to Reno. Double ceremony, Teri'i-san?"

I shook my head frantically at Teri'i. He smiled.

"If Kimi say yes?" he answered.

"This is ridiculous," I stormed. "What happened to, let's see the world, party, surf, eat, drink and be merry for tomorrow we die?"

"Kimi, Teri'i is asking you to marry him," Felice said quietly. "At least have the decency to give him an answer." My mouth dropped open in disbelief.

"This must be a dream," I decided.

"Oh, sure, why not?" I blustered. "What's the use of going to Reno if you're not getting married. Why waste a trip?"

"Double ceremony," Teri'i decided. "Where you buy ring,heah, Ito? Teri'i buy one, too."

"Perhaps in a a cracker-jack package?" I stormed home. I'd never felt so angry in my life.

"Wat wrong, Kimi?" I heard Teri'i asking Ito outside our apartment door later.

"No worry Teri'i-san. You know women. Always want romance. You sweet-talk Kimi-san tonight. Take her to a romantic movie. She'll come around. I'll show you where to buy the ring."

Chapter 19.

Return to the Tropical Palace.

"We're going home." I shouted to the gang as the final engagement we had made over the past three years was finally completed.

"Home, Mr. Emory? You mean home to Hawaii?"

My Hawaiian musicians and entertainers went wild. I felt the same way they did. It felt like a lifetime since we had left for the mainland. Several years had passed instead of the six months I had optimistically thought would be required to fulfill our contract.

I glanced around at my people. "God, they even look older," I decided. "And some of them had even gotten married, like Ito and Teri'i."

"No more touring all over the Country?" Kimi asked pointedly.

"Well, not for a while, anyway," I promised.

"Mr. Scully wants us back at the Tropical Palace. I'm finally free of committments so we can go."

I managed to get tickets for everyone on the next steamer to Honolulu. We left at the end of the week and sailed into Honolulu Harbor within a few days.

We were greeted like conquering heroes. I couldn't believe the welcome back at the Tropical Palace Hotel. Atherton Scully and his second wife Noriko had gone all out for us.

We were the guests of honor at the luau to beat all luaus.

"What gives Atherton?" I questioned my boss at a lull in the grandest Hawaiian party I had ever witnessed.

"You and the Music Director from the other hotel are economic heros in Hawaii, Winston," he laughed.

"Economic heros?" I queried.

"The market for Aloha shirts and Hawaiian souvenirs on the mainland has mushroomed unbelievably. Thanks to you and the other fellow popularizing our Islands in movies, songs, radio and band appearances all across the U. S. I don't know how you keep up the pace you do."

"Well, my family complains, all right. That they hardly ever get to see me. But I suppose it's worth it. My family will never have to worry about finances again, as long as I live. I've managed to pay for a beautiful home in New York for them. But my wife insisted they accompany us back to Hawaii. She says that Waikiki is the most beautiful place in the world. With this welcome I can hardly disagree with her."

"Those aloha shirt and ukelele sales have that much of an affect on Hawaii's economy, Atherton?" I couldn't believe it.

Atherton Scully laughed again.

"Ukelele sales alone have spawned the setup of four factories. Garment factories and souvenir factories of all kinds have been created in all of the Islands. And the tourist industry is close to rivaling sugar-cane, all thanks to you and the other fellow's Hawaiian music."

I stared at Atherton Scully in disbelief.

"All because of that sheet music we published," I tried to remain modest.

"That sheet music, the other Music Director's movies, those hundreds of appearances all over the States and the popularity of the radio show you and he had a hand in creating. I'm telling you Winston, you've turned Hawaii into a mecca for mainland and foreign visitors and their investment capital."

"See Kimi," my husband spoke quietly in my ear referring to

the conversation our boss and Mr. Scully were having at the Head Table.

"Wat Teri'i tell you? America good for both Tropical Palace entertainers and Hawaii. Everyone doing well. Hawaiians not have work only plantations anymore. Can be entertainers, work garment factories, souvenir factories, hotels."

"I guess so, Dear," I whispered back to Teri'i.

The conversation died off suddenly as a hula troupe dressed in the costumes of old suddenly moved to the stage. I gasped. The kumu hula and chantor was Aunt Auhea. The dancers were some of my childhood friends from Nanakuli.

"A special honor, Winston," Atherton Scully addressed our boss. "These authentic dancers have become very popular on the Honoulu scene. In theatres and local stage presentations, of course, not in the hotels. I thought you and your entertainers would get a kick out of viewing them. It took a substantial donation to their hula school but they agreed to perform for your homecoming."

"That's Auntie Auhea," I whispered to Teri'i. Imagine all my childhood friends are still dancing Hula Kahiko."

Auntie picked up her ipu and began to chant. A second accompianist using a temple drum began one of the sacred rhythms used for addressing the Hawaiian gods. I couldn't believe the quiet in the audience. Every eye was on the dancers and Aunt Auhea.

"I wonder if audience reaction will be different from the time you and I tried to dance the Hula Kahiko for Mr. Emory, Felice," I whispered.

"Look how spectacular the dancers have become." I watched closely. Felice was right. The dancers moved in perfect precision portraying a flow of lava down the slopes from the Halema`uma`u pit on the Big Island. They wore maile leis and had red lehua blossoms in their hair. They put on a spectacular presentation of the old Hula Kahiko.

The predominently tourist audience responded with polite

applause but without much enthusiasm. Aunt Auhea nodded to their applause and the dancers exited with another precision movement without a backward glance.

"The audience don't know what to make of that, Kimi."

"Please, Mr. Emory," someone shouted from the audience. "Won't you lead the band?"

"Only if Kimi Komo agrees to sing something for you." The audience pounded their tables and whistled imploringly. Vitori smiled and motioned for me to go up to the microphone. I obliged and Mr. Emory took over the baton of the orchestra conductor.

I managed my usual rendition of what was one of our standard selections in our repertoire. I sat down to thunderous applause but somehow I felt peculiar. I noticed Aunt Auhea watching me intently from the back of the room. Her look was not one of admiration.

"It's the contrast between the old chants and that song," I realised. "As nice that song is it really has nothing to do with Hawaiian history or culture."

"I guess Aunt Auhea has really never forgiven us for selling out, Felice?" I was surprised by the intensity of my emotions. I realised I was triggering somehow to her look of censure.

"I wonder why it bothers me so much that our old teacher still doesn't approve of what we do on stage?"

"It raises feelings to do with your mother, I bet Kimi." I gasped as I knew Felice had hit the nail on the head.

"After all these years," I thought. "Of course." My mother hadn't written to me in the three years I had been away. And I certainly wasn't going to take the first step by writing her. "How stupid to worry about what Aunt Auhea thinks. Surely there's room in Hawaii for both types of music in this day and age," I reasoned.

Still I felt uneasy for the rest of the night. There was such a difference between the old culture and what we were passing off as authentic Hawaiian music. The chant and Hula Kahiko had little if nothing in common with our modern hulas, particularly

Ito's comic hulas that the audience loved so much. I knew visitors to Hawaii and people on the mainland presumed we were representative of real Hawaiian culture. But what we were doing was only a creation of Mr. Emory and others that could make music that westerners like sound faintly Hawaiian.

I managed to quell my misgivings about what we were doing. We stayed in Hawaii for close to a year. Then Mr. Emory brought us back to California for another engagement contract. It was only supposed to be for several months.

Chapter 20.

Martial Law.

Noriko and I were about to sit down in our seats at the largest Congregational church in Hawaii when my ex-wife, Jessica, and Norman Baker unexpectedly bumped into us in the aisle. I shuddered as shock passed through my system. I hadn't seen or spoken to Jessica since she had left me for Norman Baker several years ago.

The memory of the humiliation I suffered when Jessica left me flooded my brain. I could feel the blood draining from my head.

"Take a deep breath and ground yourself, Darling." I responded automatically to Noriko's quiet voice beside me. She had been teaching me how to relax through Zen and I'd been making quite a bit of progress lately. I quickly followed her advice. Dizziness gave way to calm as I took several deep breaths in a row. I even managed to look directly at Jessica. She was staring at Noriko as if she was an abberation. Suddenly I could see some humor in the situation.

I glanced at Norman Baker. He looked remarkably well for a man of his age. I read his expression. He was only concerned for Jessica's feelings, I could tell. I gasped as I looked more closely at Jessica.

"My God, she's pregnant," I thought. "And Norman must be well into his seventies."

"Atherton," it was Noriko again. I bent down to her as she whispered something into my ear.

"Remember, Darling. The essence of Zen is unconditional love." My whole being reacted to her words. "Forgive Jessica," I knew that was what Noriko was suggesting. "After what she did?" I trembled as I remembered the humiliation I had been through. And the difficulty the divorce had caused me with my two sons. They somehow blamed me for the divorce. I still had contact but the two boys worked for Norman now and our relationship had never been the same.

"The whole congregation is watching, Dear." Noriko's quiet words caused me to look frantically around me. She was right. Every member of the wealthiest congregation on Oahu was staring at Jessica and I with undisguised curiosity.

"Aloha, Atherton." It was Baker, offering me his hand. I stared at the man fully in his eyes. His expression surprised me. I realised he was pleading with me to make peace for Jessica's sake. I hadn't expected him to be so much of a diplomat.

"Aren't you going to introduce me to your friend, Darling?" Noriko moved beside myself and Norman Baker. I realised that the last thing that both Norman and Noriko wanted was a public scene. Suddenly a sense of calm descended on me. Looking at Jessica and Noriko and their personality and age differences I realised I had got the best of the deal by far.

I realised the past didn't really matter as much as the present. Maybe the boys would understand some day. I reached out suddenly and accepted Norman's handshake. He looked enormously relieved. I could swear I saw tears in his eyes.

"Aloha Norman," I answered. "Allow me to introduce my wife Noriko."

It was my turn to look into Norman's eyes with pleading. Honolulu's elite business class had never condoned my marriage to a person of Japanese descent.

"Honored, Mrs. Scully," Norman rose to the occasion. I started as he shook Noriko's hand warmly. I realised Norman was managing to move beyond his cultural upbringing. He was publicly condoning a marriage of one of the missionary descendents to a person of another race.

I looked at Norman with new respect. I had only managed to overcome my own belief system when I'd realised how desperately I needed Noriko. I remembered how hard it was to let go of a whole lifetime of parental and societal upbringing. And Baker was from a generation older than me. Some of my righteous anger at his stealing Jessica seemed to leave me.

Norman could tell Jessica wasn't up to condoning mixed marriages, though. He gently moved her past us and into one of the aisles behind. Her expression was saying everything as she stared at Noriko. Disbelief that I had married someone of another race filled her features. I realised that she'd never be able to free herself from her dead father's belief system.

I collapsed into my seat and grabbed Noriko's hand.

"It's all right, Darling." Noriko said gently as I put my arm around her.

"You were marvelous, Atherton," she said. I gently kissed her hand. Tears came into my eyes as I felt years of baggage suddenly draining out of my system.

"Your ex-wife has good taste. Her present husband is a good man, too."

"Noriko is right," I thought unexpectedly. "Unconditional love must be the only way." It felt like a ton of bricks had been removed from my heart. By the time we rose for the end of the service Norman and Jessica had disappeared.

Members of the congregation looked at Noriko and I with new friendliness as we filed out of the Church.

"Perhaps Norman's recognition of our marriage has acted as an example to the rest of them," I thought. "He's such a leader in the community." I'd spent the last few years trying to find acceptance for Noriko's and my marriage in the very church I'd belonged to since coming to Honolulu. I spent the rest of the week wondering about odd things that happened to you in life.

"Imagine running into Norman and Jessica," I thought. "Why, they always attend the other Congregational Church. I wonder whatever possessed them to visit here. No one must have told them that Noriko and I were members of this church."

The next Sunday I wondered if they would be there again. However, neither my former wife nor her husband were present.

I was enjoying the now more friendly looks from other well-to-do, middle-aged businessmen when the sound of explosions came forcibly through the walls of the church.

"Japan is bombing Pearl Harbor," a young Marine Lieutenant came charging in and took over the altar.

"My God, the most unexpected things are happening all around me," I thought. "First, I bump into Jessica, and now bombs are dropping from the sky."

"Evacuate the church," the Marine Lieutenant ordered. Women started crying hysterically and I put my arm protectively around my slight wife. I managed to get to our home with Noriko and we listened to the radio reports with growing horror.

I tried to get through to the Tropical Palace Hotel but telephone lines were not functioning. I got into the car but quickly discovered that roads were cordoned off and there was no way to get to the Tropical Palace. I went home feeling like the end of the world had come.

The next morning at least the sirens had stopped their incessant wailing and main roads appeared to be open. I was appalled at the damage noticeable on some of the streets. The battleship Arizona had been blown up and altogether it was reported that over two thousand people had been killed. I made my way through the chaos to the Tropical Palace.

"There's someone waiting to see you, Mr. Scully," reception told me. I went into my office and a military officer stood up to his full height.

"Atherton Scully?" he demanded.

"Yes," I replied.

"I'm Admiral Thompson, Mr. Scully, Head of Navy Recreation

for Hawaii. As you know war with Japan has been declared and the military has been given explicit instructions from the Pentagon. I'm afraid I'm going to have to inform you that the Tropical Palace Hotel along with several of the other hotels have been requisitioned for the use of Navy personnel until this business is settled."

"This business, Admiral?" I gasped. Somehow I didn't connect war activities with business enterprises.

"Because the United States has declared war on Japan, and forty percent of Hawaiians are of Japanese origin, Hawaii has been placed under Martial Law."

"But what about existing business contracts, Admiral? You know the business sector here is mainly controlled by missionary descendent families of long standing originating from New England."

I tried to make my reeling brain adjust to such rapidly changing circumstances.

"And what about reservations that have already been placed?"

"You don't understand the seriousness of the situation here, Mr. Scully. All Hawaii has been placed under price and wage control. Labor will be frozen at their present work locations. I assure you that the military will pay your normal group rates for accomodation of our officers and sailors. However, all decisions affecting the Tropical Palace Hotel will now be done by military personnel. I'm afraid I must ask you to assemble your staff and then turn them over to my control."

"What about myself, Admiral? Won't you need me to assist you in running the Hotel? At least for a short while?"

"I'm afraid you'll have to take a leave of absence, Mr. Scully. I understand you're the major investor in this hotel. Don't worry, we'll keep paying the bills and you can do what you want for the duration of the war. Think of it as an extended vacation."

"I don't understand. Surely this is an unprecedented action to place businesses under direction of the military. Surely businesses are not being put under Martial Law on the mainland."

"Do I have to spell it out for you, Mr. Scully? The President is afraid of Japanese sabotage in Hawaii. We do not trust your Oriental populations, particularly the Japanese. We simply can't take a chance on their disloyalty. Believe me, anyone with close ties to the Japanese will be watched very closely."

"It's because my wife is Japanese, isn't it, that you're asking me to step down?"

"That's right, Mr. Scully. Of course we don't have any doubt about your loyalty, but Mrs. Scully's father is the President of the Japanese School Society. We can't risk what she might do out of loyalty to her father."

"Noriko's father," I gasped. "Why he's a gentleman of the highest order. And fully loyal to the United States." I shook my head. I couldn't believe what was happening to us.

"I'm sorry, Mr. Scully," the Admiral put a stop to my arguing with him.

"Just introduce me to your next-in-command. And I'll have one of my subordinates run you home in a military vehicle."

"Does this mean that all the Hawaii Sugar Plantation Association companies will be under Martial Law, too, Admiral?"

"Yes, Mr. Scully. We're not just targeting businesses with connections to Japan although they will be under particular surveillance. The threat of invasion is so severe here it's deemed necessary to control all business activity. We can't have strike and lock-out procedures interfering with the war effort. As I said earlier, all of Hawaii is being placed under Martial Law. All Civil courts have been suspended and Military courts will now be in effect. Taro and other foreign crops will be banned and agriculture geared to foods our troops can eat."

Somehow the officer's words made me feel better.

"That means Jessica and Norman will have to take orders from the U. S. Military, too," I chuckled to myself. "What revenge," I thought. My glee made me realise that I hadn't yet reached unconditional love towards Jessica and Norman.

"And if I find such a thing odious imagine how they will feel.

And what about their investments in Guatemala. Surely they won't remain unaffected by the war."

"What was I concerned with, anyway?" I addressed the stress I was feeling in my stomach, heart and throat. The Admiral was assuring me that the Tropical Palace Hotel would be full and paid-for for the duration of the war. And that our present employees would be fixed at their present rate of pay. I laughed to myself all the way out of the hotel. The military had solved my labor-management negotiations for me and fate had allowed me some revenge on Jessica and Norman.

I remembered to send a telegram cancelling Winston Emory's contract. "I guess he and his entertainers will be able to find work on the mainland," I hoped.

"Noriko," I shouted as I arrived at my front door.

"Pack up some clothes, Darling. We're going for an indefinite vacation to my properties on the outer Islands."

"Atherton," she broke into tears. "They've arrested my father and taken him off somewhere for interrogation."

"Don't worry Darling," I tried to reassure her.

"Surely they can't arrest all the Japanese people of any importance in Hawaii."

"They've arrested teachers, priests, shipping company people, fisherman, and chamber of commerce members, just because they're Japanese. They're being interned on Sand Island. They say some of them will be shipped to a detention camp on the mainland."

"Don't worry Darling. I'm sure your father will be released in due course."

Chapter 21.

On The Mainland.

I cringed at the fear in Felice's voice as she tried to stop the Military Police from arresting Ito. We were presently in Los Angeles while Winston Emory was filming a movie with us in Hollywood. We had been junketing all over the country again in a series of one-night stands and short stays as Winston Emory tried to balance his contracts with both the movie industry and big hotels.

"How dare you arrest my husband?" Felice argued, trying to hide her terror. "He's an American citizen. He was born in Hawaii."

"I'm a ukelele player with Winston Emory's band," Ito tried to explain.

"It doesn't matter Mrs. Nimura," the stocky MP pushed Felice away from Ito. She was blocking his access. The military police officer put Ito into handcuffs.

"Is that necessary, officer?" Ito complained. His face was white.

"All Japanese known to have connections with subversives are being interned in camps for the duration of the war." Another officer searched our apartment and picked up papers and any belongings that he thought were Ito's.

"Connections with subversives?" Felice went into a rage. "Just because my husband attends a Zen temple?"

"Your husband's brother attends a university in Tokyo, Mrs. Nimura. His father was caught trying to exit Honolulu on a freighter we know was heading to Japan, and the leader of his Zen temple was caught burning documents linking him to the Emperor of Japan.

"All of this has a reasonable explanation," officer," I tried to explain.

"The Japanese Emperor is the sponser of Zen and Shintoism everywhere in the world. It's a hierarchal arrangement. Ito isn't responsible for what his father does. He was asked to leave home several years ago when he chose a music career over one in accounting. Ito's brother didn't even want to attend university in Japan. He had no choice."

I cringed at the look of anger that appeared on the MP's faces at my words. I was extremely worried for Felice. She was particularly apprehensive with the birth of her first child only a few weeks away.

"I wouldn't get involved in this matter if I were you, Mrs. Fa'atua," the MP advised. "You're married to a citizen of a foreign country and we're not going to be able to lift the house arrest you've been placed under like we could for the other Hawaiian musicians. We'll have to complete our investigation of your husband's close connections to Mr. Nimura first." I choked.

"What are you going to do, officer? Place our husbands behind bars? Just for playing the ukelele and and conducting comic hulas and fire dances on American soil?"

"I assure you that anyone that has done nothing wrong will be exonerated, Mrs. Fa'atua. In the meantime I would advise you and Mrs. Nimura to seek the protection of a lawyer. If there is the slightest evidence of subversive activity on your part believe me, you'll both be joining Mr. Nimura in the internment camp at Sante Fe, New Mexico."

"Sante Fe, New Mexico," Felice shouted. "My baby is due any day. You can't take my husband so far away." She broke into sobs.

"You should have thought of that before you married a Jap, Mrs. Nimura."

"I am an American citizen," Ito yelled. "Surely I must have the right to a lawyer. I insist you let me make a call."

"Ito is the second generation of his family to be born in Hawaii," I added.

"All rights of Japanese-American citizens have been revoked by presidential order," the officer informed us.

The officers just dragged Ito out the door and slammed it shut. By the time Felice and I made it to the hallway the trio had disappeared into the elevator.

"Take care of Felice for me, Kimi-san," Ito shouted as we made it to the street just in time for the Military Police vehicle to pull out.

I grabbed onto Felice as she started to run after the car in the street.

"Felice, you have to think of your baby," I told her. "Ito will be all right, I'm sure. After all this is America."

I dragged her back upstairs.

"Where is Teri'i?" I wondered frantically. The last I'd seen of him had been several days before when the announcement had come over the radio about the bombing of Pearl Harbor. He had suddenly left the apartment despite my arguing against it.

"Teri'i, you could be deported back to Tahiti," I pleaded. "Don't go out until we get your landed immigrant status confirmation from Honolulu?"

Teri'i hadn't come back that night. The Hawaiian personnel of our whole review had been immediately investigated the next day. We'd been placed under house arrest.

"No worry, Kimi," was all he'd tell me on the telephone, when he called. "Teri'i has someting he has to do. I'll explain when get back."

"Get back from where?" Only a click had answered my question.

Felice was hysterical for the rest of the day. I took her to a doctor and he prescibed a sedative for her. About 8:00 our apartment door opened with a key.

"Teri'i," I stared in complete horror at my husband. He was dressed in a U.S. Army uniform.

"Teri'i enlist, Kimi," he explained. French Polynesia now under control of Free French forces. Military Police say all right for Teri'i join army. America good fo Teri'i. Must pay back now."

"Teri'i, Ito's been arrested. He's been sent off to Sante Fe, New Mexico for the duration of the war."

"Must be mistake, Kimi. You see. Dey release wen dey find out truth." I hugged him close.

Teri'i, you could get killed or something. What are you doing getting involved in this war?"

"No choice, Kimi. America good to Teri'i. Must prove loyalty now or return Tahiti. Vitori no want leave Kimi."

Felice came out of her bedroom and stared at Teri'i in horror. We both fell into each other's arms sobbing.

"Teri'i no have time, Kimi. Must report in morning boot camp."

"What about Ito?" Felice asked. "How are Kimi and I going to get him out of that internment camp?"

"Get lawyer, Felice. Teri'i pay. Army send money to Kimi every month. Teri'i sign. Must be mistake dey lock him up."

"What am I going to do about the band now? Mr. Emory's going to keep taking the show on the road in between fulfilling his movie contracts. I had better resign and stay here so we can meet when you get leave. That way I'll be able to help Felice and the baby until Ito comes back."

"Not wit war, Kimi. You, Felice stay wit band. At least be wit people you know. Teri'i come to Kimi wen he get leave. Ito return wen he released."

Winston Emory couldn't do anything for Ito either. "I'm sorry, Felice. I've tried all my contacts. Besides, maybe it's safer for him in that internment camp. You know how much propaganda is going around California about Japanese people."

"But Mr. Emory. My baby is going to be born anytime? How am I going to manage without Ito."

"You come with the band, Felice. You and Kimi, like Teri'i told you. I've got a whole series of one night stands set up all over the country. I'll put you on the payroll in Ito's place. That's about all I can do for him right now. When you feel up to it after the baby's birth, you can rejoin us as one of the dancers."

"Thanks Mr. Emory," I managed for Felice. "At least that way Felice won't be all alone."

Felice had a six pound ten ounce boy the next morning. She named the baby, Ito Jr. The Sante Fe internment camp that Ito was in wouldn't even let her speak to him.

"We'll pass the word along to him, Mrs. Nimura," the officer in charge assured her as I took the phone from Felice. She couldn't speak she was crying so hard.

"Is Ito Nimura all right?" I demanded. "So far we haven't gotten as much as a letter from him." I explained how Felice and I would be travelling all over with Winston Emory's band.

"It'll be a while before we can permit our charges to write letters, Mrs. Fa'atua. Just keep me advised of your whereabouts. I assure you I'll keep Mr. Nimura informed about his wife and baby."

We rejoined the band in New Orleans three weeks later. Fortunately Ito Jr. was blessed with the same happy disposition as his father and seemed not to suffer any bad effects from being driven all over the country.

The war years went with a whirl. Teri'i managed to meet us several times the first year until he was sent overseas to serve in Italy. The last time I saw him I was so scared I could hardly talk. They'd transferred him to the paratroops corp and there was some danger he might be dropped close to enemy lines.

"No worry, Kimi," he said after our love-making. "Teri'i dodge bullet like flaming torch in fire dance."

I laughed. He always had such a spirit of optimism that things would work out.

We even got back to Oahu again but without Winston Emory. He took the odd vacation and we were free to entertain the troops both on the mainland and in Hawaii.

My daughter Teri'iana was born in Honolulu, exactly nine months after my final visit with Teri'i before he went overseas. She was perfect in every way.

"She look just like Teri'i, Kimi," Tutu remarked in awe as she visited in the hospital with my brother Kimo. I couldn't believe Kimo's height. He was over six feet four. He was too young for the draft but was determined to enlist if the war went on long enough. Mother still wouldn't see me.

"Mother still not forgive, Kimi." Tutu explained. "She say Winston Emory music only fake Hawaii. Big on radio now, and movies, Hawaii and mainland. Sell out old culture."

"For Pete's sake, Tutu," I managed through my tears. "I suppose Mother is right but do you know how many people enjoy the kind of music the band plays? Especially with the war years. People have a right to enjoy themselves even if the music is not authentic."

"Tutu no get involved Kimi. She wait. One day you, mother understand each other." Only we didn't.

A steady stream of letters followed me all over the States and Hawaii from the war zone in Europe.

"Teri'i so happy, Kimi," he wrote. "Now two Kimi's, you and little Teri'iana. Can't wait to see. Always in heart. Maybe war be over soon."

Chapter 22.

Forced Changes.

By 1944 I was beginning to believe that the war was never going to be over. Letters from Teri'i became more and more scary. It wasn't what he said, it was what he didn't say. Missing from his letters was his usual optimism.

Then two years after the birth of our daughter the thing I'd been fearing most in the world happened.

Felice answered the knock at the door. We were back on Oahu dancing hula for the troops with the band while Mr. Emory was having a vacation.

"Mrs. Teri'i Fa'atua?" inquired the uniformed telegram person.

"I'm Mrs. Fa'atua," I told the young man, fear gripping my heart like a vice. I ripped open the envelope.

"Regret to inform you that Sergeant Teri'i Fa'atua was seriously wounded in action in Salerno, on the afternoon of June 23, 1944. He is being transferred to an intensive care unit, the whereabouts of which we cannot reveal due to the war. We will keep you informed by telegram as to his status."

The telegram was signed by the State Department.

I collapsed into Felice's arms. I dimly remember Ito Jr. watching from the bedroom as Felice and I shook with sobs.

It was weeks and several telegrams later until I knew that

Teri'i was not going to die. It took him until December of 1944 to be well enough to returned to Hawaii. All that time and I'd not received any letter from him.

Felice and I had a wild celebration after we opened the telegram that arrived on Christmas Eve.

"Pleased to inform you that Sergeant Teri'i Fa'atua will be arriving in Honolulu Harbor by troop transport on Boxing Day."

"Felice," I questioned my dearest friend after we had stopped celebrating. "How come Teri'i hasn't written. And why I haven't received any details as to the nature of his wounds? You don't suppose there's something seriously wrong still, like brain injury or something?"

"Don't be ridiculous, Kimi. It's just the war. Everything is classified these days. Come on let's go out and buy you and Teri'iana new dresses for Vitori's homecoming."

"If only Ito Sr. could be here. Come on, let's tell the gang at the Tropical Palace. They'll all want to be there when Teri'i comes home."

"No, Felice. I want to meet him by myself. There's got to be some reason he hasn't written. We can celebrate with the gang later."

I barely made it through Christmas Day. I was so apprehensive about my husband. I kept sensing something was terribly wrong. I left Teri'iana with Felice as Boxing Day finally arrived. I drove down to the pier by myself in Teri'i's car that I had brought over from the mainland.

"He'll be so happy to see it," I thought. "It's still in the condition it was in when he left. It's hardly been used."

By the time I got to the pier the Hospital ship had already docked. I walked up the ramp with the crowd of anxious relatives and managed to reach a uniformed guard with a list of names in his hand.

"I'm Mrs. Fa'atua, Sergeant Teri'i Fa'atua's wife," I introduced myself.

"Do you have some identification, Mrs. Fa'atua?"

I showed the guard my drivers license. The guard ran down his alphabetical list.

"Mrs. Fa'atua, I've found him. Your husband is one deck down waiting for you in the lounge area. Take that staircase down."

My heart pounded frantically as I descended the steps. I reached the door of the lounge and peered intensely through the glass. I gasped as the lounge seemed to be full of soldiers and sailors who had been badly wounded. Some were on crutches and others were in wheelchairs. I winced as I frantically searched for Teri'i. Many of the servicemen had missing parts of their bodies and some were badly scarred on their faces.

Then I spotted Teri'i. He was sitting quietly by himself in a large armchair in one of the corners. I moved towards him scanning him all over in great anxiety.

"Why isn't he recognising me?" I thought. "He's staring right at me. And why is he wearing those dark sunglasses inside the ship?"

I made it right up to Teri'i and stopped myself suddenly before I grabbed him. He still was showing no sign of knowing who I was.

"Teri'i," I cried out as I spotted the scar on his forehead. It was bright red like it had just healed over.

"Kimi," Teri'i's face went into his huge beaming smile. "Kimi," he stood up and I threw myself into his open arms. We kissed and held each other tight for what seemed an eternity. Finally Teri'i loosened his grip on my body.

"Kimi, someting you need know."

"Sure, we'll have time later. You can tell me everything, then. Let's just get out of here."

"Kimi, Teri'i blind," he said sadly.

I shuddered and then fought not to reveal my shock and horror. My husband looked very anxious about how I was reacting.

"That's why you didn't write?"

"Want tell Kimi in person. Teri'i not know if Kimi want blind husband."

"For God's sake," I cried out. "Of course Kimi still want husband, blind or otherwise."

Teri'i took me into his arms again and hugged me very close for a long time. Tears streamed down both our faces.

"It's all right, Darling," I tried to reassure him. You're alive and back with us again. That's all that matters."

Teri'i smiled but I could see he wasn't really convinced.

"Teri'i's name in fo Seeing-Eye dog, Kimi," he said choking back his tears. "Army doctor say dog act as eyes fo Teri'i." I sensed that Teri'i really wanted to believe the doctor's words but wasn't completely convinced.

"Of course," I repressed my own fears and tried to sound hopeful. "Come on, let's get out of this medical atmosphere. Teri'iana, Felice and Ito Junior are waiting at home to see you."

"Kimi, Teri'i no do fire dance now, how he support family?"

"For God's sake," I exclaimed. "There's more to life than fire dancing. Maybe my mother might speak to us again now that you're not dancing fake Hawaiian."

I managed a slight smile as Teri'i chuckled slightly.

"Kimi right," he sighed. Tears came to his eyes again. He grasped my arm tightly.

"Take Teri'i home, Kimi. Can't wait meet Teri'iana, Felice and Ito Jr."

"They're beautiful children. Just like their fathers."

I drove Teri'i home in his car. My heart felt sad as I looked at the expression on his face as I manoevered the large car through the streets of Honolulu. I could tell Teri'i was thinking that he'd never drive the car again, himself.

"I've got to get him some counselling about this," I silently acknowledged to myself, realising the enormity of Teri'i's pain. He was trying to put on a brave front but I could sense his feelings of helplessness.

"I'll phone Tutu in Hilo, soon," I decided as we arrived at the apartment I was renting with Felice. "Tutu always knows what to do."

Felice was waiting in the living room with the children.

"Aloha Teri'i," she cried as we entered the door.

I stepped backward as both children eagerly toddled towards us. Ito Jr. was a little over three years old now and Teri'iana was just two. Teri'i knelt down as the children reached him. He gathered both of them up in his arms and hugged them close.

"Daddy," Teri'iana cried, "Daddy." It was the first time she had ever said that word. Tears were running down everyones eyes. I grasped Teri'i by his elbow and guided him over to the chesterfield. He collapsed into it with the children tumbling on to his lap.

Felice looked at me in horror as she grasped that Teri'i was blind. I put my fingers to my lips and shook my head warning her not to say anything. I realised how super sensitive Teri'i was about the situation.

"Teri'iana, Ito, beautiful children," Teri'i commented. He ran his hands gently over their faces.

Teri'i so glad to be home," he sobbed.

When I got up the next morning Teri'i had the exact number of spaces from room to room and furniture to furniture mapped out in his mind. I realised I'd better stop moving furniture around like I was accustomed to doing.

"Your memory is still magnificent," I congratulated him. He was able to navigate our apartment like a sighted person.

"Army orderly teach Teri'i how memorize steps, Kimi."

"You always were a good learner, Dear."

After breakfast Teri'i had me call the Army Unit that handled the compensatory training for the handicapped. He insisted I get through to someone who could tell him how long it would be before he could get a Seeing-Eye dog.

"Tell him his name is already on the list, Mrs. Fa'atua. We'll have a dog for him within a month."

I relayed the news to Teri'i.

Our friends at the Tropical Palace quickly learned about

Teri'i's blindness. They organised a party for him a week after he'd returned.

It was a good thing that Teri'i couldn't see the expressions on people's faces. They sounded cheerful but their looks, when they thought I wasn't looking, said everything. Many of our friends sang and played instruments but they couldn't get Teri'i to join in. I tried to look confident and optimistic for the sake of Teri'i and Teri'iana but tears escaped several times during the evening. I knew things would never be the same again.

It was extremely difficult for Teri'i. I knew he hated it when I went off to entertain at the Tropical Palace.

The State Department gave Teri'i a handicapped pension. But he was determined to find something he could do that would allow him to feel like he was supporting his family again. He insisted I stay on with Winston Emory's troupe of entertainers. So for much of the year I danced my way through the hulas and sang the romantic songs that had become the standard menu for troop shows and soldiers returning from and leaving for the front in Europe.

Teri'i graduated from the Seeing-Eye Dog Training Program in September of 1945 and brought one of the most intelligent dogs I had ever met home to live with us. Her name was Chelsey and she was one of the biggest Doberman's I had ever seen. She spent her time watching. She watched things that Teri'i might run into. She watched for cars before she would let Teri'i cross a road. She even watched over other members of the family. I was willing to bet that the creator of the Doberman breed programmed them to watch over everything in this world.

With the dog Teri'i was able to move about Oahu almost like a sighted person.

"Army right, Kimi. Chelsey do seeing for Teri'i." Some of my husband's old optimism returned to him as he realised that with the dog he could do many of the things he did before his blindness. We went on hikes and some of the boys in the band got Teri'i to surf again. All he needed was someone to stay close and tell him when to turn. Teri'i took over most of the housework, the cooking and food shopping. The big Doberman's devotion and love to our entire family seemed a great source of healing.

However Teri'i was greatly disappointed that no one would hire him to do paid work of any kind.

"They all tell Teri'i same, Kimi. Take Government pension, enjoy life. No one willing take chance on blind person."

"It's their loss," I told him but I could tell Teri'i wasn't convinced.

Ito was released from the Sante Fe internment camp two weeks after the end of the war. We all went to meet the steamer that was bringing him back to Honolulu Harbor. Hope almost faded completely as the whole ship seemed to empty before Ito made his way down the entrance ramp. I grabbed Ito Jr. and Teri'iana as Felice rushed forward into her husband's arms.

"Ito-san so happy to be back," Ito sobbed as he finally released Felice and hugged his now four year old son against his chest. He glanced at Teri'iana and Teri'i and even more tears filled his eyes.

"Your daughter looks just you, Teri'i-san," he sobbed as all of us hugged each other in an incredible emotional outpouring. Never before had I felt so much pain and joy at the same time.

"We stay in Honolulu, Kimi," Ito announced the next day. "Ito-san, Felice-san never return to mainland again, Kimi. Too many bad memories."

I glanced at Ito. He'd aged in the four years he was imprisoned. He was no longer chubby and his hair was prematurely streaked with grey. I somehow managed to keep my tears from spilling out.

"They need a ukelele and steel-guitar player at the Tropical Palace, Hotel, Ito," I managed. Winston Emory is the Music Director again."

"Good Kimi. Ito-san write many Hawaiian ukelele and steel guitar pieces while in internment camp. Maybe even write comic-hula again someday, but don't feel up to it now."

I stuck it out for a year doing the old songs at the Tropical Palace Hotel. But something was drastically wrong. Due to people's attitudes towards the handicapped no one would give Teri'i a job. The Institute For The Blind wanted him to run one of their magazine stands but Teri'i didn't want to be an object of pity from the public.

On top of that, no matter how I tried, I couldn't manage enthusiasm for the type of music we were playing any longer. Fewer and fewer locals were coming to our shows. It was mainly the tourists that filled the lounge of the Tropical Palace Hotel night after night.

One weekend Tutu came to visit Teri'i, Teri'iana and I.

"Kimi have black marks under eyes," she said accusingly when Teri'i took Chelsey and Teri'iana out to the drug store for some ice cream. I fell into her arms.

"Tutu, I don't know what's wrong," I sobbed. "I just don't want to go on the stage anymore. The music and dancing doesn't make me happy the way it used to."

"Kimi, Tropical Palace music fake Hawaii like Mother say all dese years. Make Teri'i sad now, too. He can no longer do fire dance. You two need change. Maybe move from Oahu."

Intuitively I knew Tutu was right.

"But we can't leave Felice and Ito, Tutu. They're the only family Teri'i and I have besides you and Kimo."

"Felice, Ito, understand, Kimi. You, Teri'i, Teri'iana come wit Tutu to Hilo. Kimo need help wit orchid farm. Doing well, but Kimo have work night and day. He should be looking fo wife. Having fun. Not work all time like Tutu and mother. Kimi, you and your mother do ho'oponopono. Reach understanding, forgive."

"How is that possible, Tutu?" My emotions overwhelmed me. Suddenly I wanted more than anything in the world to go to Hilo with Tutu but I didn't see how I could. I'd have to admit that my mother was right. That I'd wasted the last decade of my life instead of doing something meaningful. I felt like such a failure.

"Tutu arrange Kimi. Get Kahuna. Conduct ho'oponopono. Everything be all right. Tutu know."

"Maybe Teri'i could help with the orchids, Tutu. It's amazing what he's able to do with Chelsey's help. It's just that no one wants to take a chance and employ someone with a handicap."

"Kimi tired singing Hapa-Haole songs. Teri'i need be helpful. Both need do wat is in heart."

I realised Tutu was right. Deep within I knew my heart was trying to tell me that there was more to life than the "Happy Hour" at the Tropical Palace Hotel.

"Hilo need teachers, Kimi. Tidal wave destroy homes, school. Mainland teachers leave. Mother, Tutu, Kimo need help with orchids. Many Hawaiian children in Hilo want learn Hula Kahiko. Maybe Kimi show how?"

"Maybe I could get back into teaching, Tutu. I'd probably have to update but there's a college campus on the Big Island. Maybe it is possible? But do you think mother can find it in her heart to forgive me?"

Sobs shook my body. Everything Tutu said made sense to me. I realised how much we needed a change. How cut off we felt from anything of any importance.

"Tutu know it be ok, Kimi. Follow Aloha witin. Only way."

I had a long talk with Teri'i. After his initial surprise he seemed to think it was a good idea.

"Teri'i want go Hilo, Kimi. Need be working. Teri'i want help support Kimi and Teri'iana. Want do someting more than laze around house."

Then we talked to Ito and Felice.

"Ito, my grandmother wants us to come join her in Hilo. Maybe Teri'i will be able to work on Mother's Orchid Farm. Do something worthwhile again. I know it sounds funny after all the years I swore I'd never live in a remote area. But somehow it sounds right for us."

"Ito-san understand," our old friend replied.

"Felice and I didn't want to tell you but my brother wants me to come for an extended visit to Japan. In my heart I know I should go there, at least for a while."

"They say there's a growing market for slack-key guitar artists in Japan, Ito. I understand there's several Hawaiian groups touring over there right now."

"I understand, too, Kimi." It was Felice. She had tears in her eyes. "It'll be hard, I know. After all we've been through but I think it's important for Ito Jr. and Teri'iana to find out something about their cultures. Ito Jr's been asking me a lot of questions about Japan lately. Ever since we got those letters and pictures from Ito's brother. What about you, Teri'i, ever think of going back to Tahiti?"

"Brudders write, Felice. But say no come back. Dey want visit here, instead. Now even Tahiti Government controlled by rich French and part Tahitians. Frame Tahitian leader, Pouovana O'opa wen try bring in law dat make rich pay income tax. He now in jail in France. Brudders all leeving in crowded shanty-towns. All coastline Tahiti, Moorea being turned into resorts fo very rich."

We hugged Ito and Felice.

A month later I left the Tropical Palace. Teri'i, Chelsey, Teri'iana and I took a steamer to Hilo. The steamer people let our Doberman on because she was a Seeing-Eye dog. As the steamer arrived in Hilo harbor it stopped raining and a double rainbow lit up the sky over the old buildings that had survived the recent tidal wave.

"It's going to be all right, Darling," I told my husband as Kimo and Tutu worked their way up the ramp to where I was standing on deck. Teri'i was looking a little doubtful.

"There's a double rainbow in the sky."

Tutu and I collapsed in each other's arms. Kimo grabbed Teri'iana and lifted her joyously up in his arms. Then he turned to Teri'i and hugged him warmly. I couldn't believe Kimo was a grown man.

"And all without my being there for him," I thought with guilt.

"Mahalo for coming, Teri'i," he said. "You can't imagine how much I need help with the orchids." Teri'i beamed.

The rainbow is an omen, isn't it Tutu?" I managed between tears of joy. Somehow I knew it was going to be all right.

Kimo piled our bags into the trunk of his old car and Teri'i, Teri'iana, Chelsey and I went into the back seat. I couldn't believe the damage the recent tidal wave had caused. The Hilo waterfront looked like a war zone.

"It'll be years before Hilo gets back to normal again," I said.

"We're a hardy lot around here, Kimi," Kimo replied. You'll be surprised how quickly the community gets itself back on it's feet."

We pulled into a farm that looked a lot better than the old house that our family used to rent near Nanakuli. A large house stood in a field surrounded by sheds covered in glass and plastic. Fields of multi-colored orchids were visible growing behind the fence.

I looked at the old house in consternation. Somewhere inside I knew my mother was waiting.

"Teri'i, Teri'iana, come with me," Kimo ordered as we got out of the car. "I'll show you the pony I've bought for Teri'iana. He's out by the barn."

Our daughter's and Teri'i's faces lit up like a Christmas tree. Kimo led them off towards the barn.

I followed Tutu into the house. She paused at the front door and turned to me.

"Kimi. Kahuna here to do ho`oponopono. You, mother must forgive."

I looked at Tutu in shock.

"We're in the living room," a booming voice informed us as we entered the kitchen.

I started as I entered my mother's living room. It was like I had been transported back in time. An aged Hawaiian was standing in the center of the room dressed in the clothes of old Hawaii. He was wearing a a rough woven cloak. In his hand he held a carved wooden stick with the image of a god at the top.

I glanced closely at the carved image. From my childhood training at Aunt Auhea's hula halau I knew the image was a representation of the goddess Hina. She was the Hawaiian goddess of all things of female energy. My heart pounded as I realised I was in the presence of one of the few remaining Kahunas on the Big Island. Chills ran up and down my spine as the Kahuna started chanting in Hawaiian.

"Thank Heavens Tutu is here with me," I thought. She looked at me reassuredly as I gave her a searching look.

"Kimi, this Naoni Kekela," she said.

The old fellow said something in a commanding tone.

"Kimi Fa'atua, be seated," I translated the Kahuna's instructions. I winced as I hardly remembered the Hawaiian language from my childhood. I quickly sat down on the wooden chair he was pointing to in the middle of the room.

"We will begin the Ho`oponopono now," he chanted solemnly.

I found the courage to glance around the room. My eyes fell on a lady in the corner dressed in a tapa dress. A lei was around her shoulders and red lehua flowers were intertwined in her hair. I recognised my mother with a shock.

Tears came to my eyes as I realised she had aged considerably in the ten years we hadn't been speaking. Mother was staring at me looking very serious. As I returned her gaze I could feel considerable pain around my heart.

"We will do a greeting prayer," I translated the Kahuna's chanting again.

"Lower your gaze," he instructed. "We are requesting the presence of the goddess Hina in this house. She presides over Ho`oponoponos dealing with female energy."

I knew better than to say anything as my mother stared intensely at me. Her gaze seemed to be going right through me.

I listened closely to the words of the Kahuna. I was having trouble translating everything he said. My heart increased its beat again as he went into what appeared to me to be some kind of trance following a particularly long flow of chanting. The whole room seemed to be filling with some kind of an electrical energy.

The Kahuna's chanting intensified. His eyes were closed as if he were channeling some kind of presence into the room.

Suddenly a blinding flash of lightning lit up the room. A deafening bang from thunder struck almost at the same time.

"Be still," the Kahuna warned us in Hawaiian. "The goddess Hina is present in this room and the goddess Pele is also present." He uttered what I realised was a greeting chant with his voice alternating in volume eerily. I could feel a flow of cold air against my face and body.

"Hina directs that we must search for the source of the discord between this woman and her daughter," the Kahuna instructed.

"It is my daughter's fault," my mother said in a blaming voice.

"She has devoted her adult years to defiling our history and showing our sacred chant and dance in public. Kimi has betrayed the sacred trust given to our family by Pele to preserve and safeguard the old ways."

"Is this so?" the aged Kahuna asked me in Hawaiian.

"Dancing hula for tourists was a means of earning the money to pay my school fees so I could become a teacher," I tried to explain.

The energy in the room seemed to thicken as I blurted out what even seemed to me to be a weak excuse. Then another roar of thunder and flash of lightning happened.

"The goddess Pele is very displeased," the Kahuna interpreted.

"I'm sorry," I apologised. "I didn't realise it was wrong to modernize the old dances and chants."

"Not just modernize them, Kimi," my mother protested in an angry tone. "I watch some of the dances and songs you did for that Winston Emory from the mainland. He changed and distorted our history, values and lifestyle. You and others like you have done serious harm to the true Hawaiian culture."

"Thank Goodness mother never saw the Princess Poo-poo`-

ly cover," I thought. Another crash of thunder informed me that the goddess Pele had probably seen it.

I despaired. My heart felt extremely heavy and painful.

"There's no way mother is going to forgive me," I thought, "let alone the goddesses Pele and Hina. I shouldn't have brought Teri'i and Teri'iana here to her house."

"Kimi not only one at fault," Tutu interrupted her voice very serious. "Mother have Kimi dance Hula Kahiko and practice old ways all childhood. Kimi rebel finally when tink she get opportunity to make someting more of herself."

My mother reacted violently to Tutu's words.

"How dare you say that Mother?" she cried out in Hawaiian. "You know my father left us the sacred trust of preserving the chants and Hula Kahiko of our family."

Another boom of thunder crashed around us even louder than the others. The living room window disintegrated with a crash. Glass pieces fell all over the floor.

"See, Pele agrees," Mother decreed.

"Be silent," the Kahuna commanded.

"Hina is telling me that it is she and not Pele that presides over Ho`oponoponos. She does not like the negativity in this room. The goddess reminds me that it is the present and that we can not change the past. She reminds me that the Hawaiian way is one of Aloha. It is a good sign that Kimi has brought her husband and daughter back to the family and that Teri'i wants to help, rather than rely on an American pension. Hina commands that Kimi and her mother reach forgiveness."

"Kimi has apologised. It is her mother's turn. She must forgive immediately or Hina will destroy the current orchid crop with a flood of rain and hail."

"I'm sorry," I cried out. "I promise never to dance fake hula or chant anything other than ancient oli again."

"Perhaps I was a little too demanding of such a young child," my mother seemed to reconsider.

My heart felt like it was going to burst with pain.

"Perhaps Kimi would not have been so stubborn if I had allowed her more free time to play with friends."

"Mother finally reach understanding," Tutu exclaimed. "Tutu wait so long fo you."

I sat completely without moving as the Kahuna raised some kind of carved stick and chanted in the old way. I realised he was clearing the air of negative energy and calling on the Hawaiian gods of old to bless the orchid farm and Teri'i's and my coming.

The old Hawaiian gentleman continued chanting in Hawaiian. I realised he was asking the goddess Pele for forgiveness for me and Teri'i and our betrayal of Hawaiian culture by singing and dancing the fake Hawaiian music of Winston Emory. He also asked Hina to forgive my mother for being too zealous in demanding that a young child devote herself entirely to the Hula Kahiko and the ways of the people of old.

"Kimi Fa'atua," the Kahuna switched to English.

I could feel a cool breeze flowing slowly all over my face and body again.

"What is your promise to Hina and Pele?"

"I'll never sing Hapa-haole songs or dance comic hula again," I promised, turning towards my aging mother. I'm sorry I'm such a failure."

"Goddess Hina say no failure, Kimi." It was Tutu interfering. "Teri'i, Teri'iana good people. Lots of Aloha in heart. Goddess Hina always happy when one of her wahines or kanes bring her good people."

"Tutu is right, Kimi, at last you've come home to us," mother sobbed. Her disapproving expression had left her face. Tears were running down her face.

I felt the cool breeze intensify and then suddenly move away from my presence.

"At last you reach forgiveness, Mrs. Kai`ika," the Kahuna sounded happier. "The goddess Pele accepts your apology, Kimi. She asks you to join one of the Hula Kahiko schools in Hilo for repentence. There are many children to teach."

I nodded.

"I'm sure I'll remember the steps with a little practice."

The old gentleman chanted something in Hawaiian again for several minutes.

"With this seawater from Hilo Bay this wahine and her family are freed from past transgression," I translated his words. He put a few drops on my head, mother's and Tutu's. Then he sprayed a little water around the room.

"And this family is freed from the negativity of years of disagreement."

The Kahuna shook drops of seawater over the floorboards of the living room. I felt warmth replace the pain around my heart.

"Welcome to Hilo, Mrs. Fa'atua," the old gentleman added as he turned to leave. "By the way I'm the kumu hulu for a halau of children. We meet every Thursday and Monday nights in the Hilo Church hall. Perhaps you and your daughter would like to join us?"

"Mahalo nui loa," I said gratefully as the old fellow left. Just then Teri'iana. Chelsey, Teri'i and Kimo came rushing in to the living room.

"Mommy, you have to come and see my new pony," Teri'iana cried. His name is Pueo."

"Teri'i's memorized the number of steps from the flower sheds to the house already," Kimo said in amazement.

"Teri'iana, this is your grandmother. Teri'i this is my mother," I took my husbands and daughter's hands and went over to my mother. She stared at Teri'i and Teri'iana in wonderment.

"Kimi, you've returned to us. And Tutu is right. You've brought us this beautiful child and this handsome man with you. At last our family is back together."

All four of us fell into each others arms.

As soon as I felt the strength of my mother's hugs I knew we had come where we should be. My heart pounded with emotion as Tutu joined in. Kimo smiled at us from across the room.

"Now mother and Kimi understand each other," Tutu sighed. "Tutu wait so long."

"You should have seen that thunderstorm," Kimo exclaimed. "I was sure the orchids were going to be ruined but not even a drop of rain hit them. It was most peculiar. By the way what happened to that window?"

BVG